Who is Fiengus Longfinger?

G. W. Witherspoon

G. W. Witherspoon

ISBN: 1500638188
ISBN-13: 978-1500638184

DEDICATION

This book is for:
Alfie, Jacob and Alice.

G. W. Witherspoon

G. W. Witherspoon

ACKNOWLEDGMENTS

Thanks to my partner, Eilidh, for putting up with me typing, swearing and creating a mess of paper, books and concentric coffee ring stains on all available surfaces. Thanks to the kids for listening to the story as it was being written, giving ideas and laughing appropriately. And of course thanks to everyone who has influenced and inspired me, the list is of course too extensive.

1 A DILEMMA

Fiengus Longfinger sat and stared out of his living room window and thought to himself, "What will I do with my life?" This was a question that he had been asking himself a lot lately. He was an ordinary man in almost every respect except in respect to his unordinary finger. It was a very long finger. This in itself is not really a remarkable thing, but Fiengus' finger was made so long by the gods themselves. And this made it a special finger. However, the origin and length of the finger seemed to be the only special thing about it; as far as anyone could tell the finger did nothing, except those things an ordinary finger might do. This gift and the question of what it actually was provided the source of the sadness and existential quandary which he found himself in. He just didn't know what to do. And to make things worse he wasn't even sure what an existential quandary was.

The idea that he was in one came from his friend Professor Helmsman, who he had been chatting to earlier about his predicament. "Fiengus," he had said, "you're in what we call an existential quandary. It's very common, especially with those with special gifts, like your finger." Fiengus had replied that he didn't know what he meant, and when Professor Helmsman had explained that it basically meant that he didn't know who he was or what he should do with his life, he felt no better about the whole thing. Fiengus knew these things, what did it matter that he called it an existential quandary. He had left not long after that, feeling more confused about his confusing situation and returned home. Which was where he now was, looking out of his window.

His problems were made worse by a letter that had arrived that morning. At around 9 in the morning the letter had arrived from the Mayor of Von Dufflestein, requesting Fiengus come and see him at 4 in the afternoon. A meeting with the Mayor was one thing, but the last sentence which had said, 'We desperately need your assistance in a matter beyond our capabilities: you are our only hope!' had only made his feeling worse than ever. He had absolutely no idea what it related to and why *he* was the only hope. Fiengus was, by his own admission, a bit of a layabout, caused not by being lazy, but simply from not knowing what to do. His whole life was like this and he felt that it needed a purpose, something to give meaning to it. The summons from the Mayor he hoped might provide exactly this, but it was a distant hope; the Mayor was not renowned for his professionalism or for giving people anything much of any worth to do.

It was quarter to 4 now and Fiengus wanted nothing more than to hide. However, one thing Fiengus wasn't was a coward. He put on his coat, hat and bespoke gloves and left the house.

2 THE MEETING WITH THE MAYOR

Fiengus drove through the streets of Von Dufflestein, in the direction of the Mayor's office. The roadways were predominantly cobbled in the town, which was fairly large, being once a trading port, of some importance, in its hay day. Dominating the skyline of the town was the University, which was world famous for its groundbreaking research. The surrounding environs of the town were mainly rural, resplendent with beautiful hills and mountains with crystal clear rivers cutting through them, vast forests of great and ancient trees and fine arable land which was tilled by the local farmers. To the north of the town lay the sea, so vast and crystalline and once of major importance to the town. The air of the town was filled with the scent of the salty sea when the wind blew in from the north and the scent of pine trees when blowing from the south. It was a wonderful place to live, thought Fiengus, and he was grateful to do so.

It was not far to the Mayor's office and he arrived in good time. He entered the large building, which had a very grand front, decorated with columns and a mural depicting the founding fathers of the town. Fiengus gave this little heed and entered hastily into the reception area, seemingly intent on getting on with business. "Have a seat, the Mayor is expecting you," said the receptionist.

Fiengus had just sat down when the Mayor burst into the hallway. He was a portly man, wearing a suit that may have fit years ago and was sweating profusely. His greying hair was very unkempt, and looked like it had been something blowing in the wind prior to attaching itself to the man's head. The Mayor gave the immediate impression of someone who was stressed and had nothing in the way of coping strategies to deal with it. "Why did you not tell me he was here!" he cried at the receptionist. "This way, quickly, we have much to discuss," he said as he ushered Fiengus into his office.

The office was a mess with papers strewn across the Mayor's desk and a general atmosphere of nervous tension filled the air. Through the windows, which dominated much of the far wall, it was possible to gaze out over the whole town and capture it within the frame, giving it a portraiture like appearance. This beautiful view was in stark contrast to the office. The mess on the desk flew suddenly into the air as the Mayor seemed to search desperately for something. "Take a seat Fiengus," said a voice from behind. Fiengus turned to see a man he recognised, but could not recall from where.

He began to sit down, when the Mayor screamed, "Not there you fool!" He then rushed over and grabbed something from the chair and in doing so knocked the chair over. Fiengus was unsure whether he should pick up the chair or leave it as the Mayor had knocked it down and should pick it up himself he felt; on the other hand he was the Mayor and was possibly due extra respect in these sorts of situations. Before he could come to a conclusion the Mayor whisked him over to a large table, upon which there was a map with coloured pins dotted in it.

"This map," said the Mayor, "shows the locations of the *Instance*s."

"That's what we are calling them," added the familiar stranger.

"Yes, that is what we have decided. It's a working title, but seems popular with everyone here. What do you think, eh Fiengus?" asked the Mayor, who was staring expectantly at him.

Fiengus had no idea to what the name referred, but did not want to seem like he wasn't paying attention. "Yes, that is a good name," he ventured, the Mayor did not change his expression of expectation. "Makes it all very clear; *Instances*, why yes of course." The Mayor seemed pleased by this, but only momentarily.

He then began to throw his arms in the air and wail out, "What are we to do about this? It's confirmed that they should be called *Instances*; this is grim news!" The Mayor then threw himself down into the chair that Fiengus had just picked up, having felt he needed a distraction from the Mayors awkward display.

The stranger approached Fiengus and directed him to the map. "Look, Fiengus, at what this is doing to the Mayor, he's distraught. We need to sort this out immediately. Can you do it?"

"I'm not sure," he replied, which caused the Mayor to wail even louder. "I mean, I'm not sure what these *Instance*s are, they need investigating I am sure, but their nature at the moment remains a mystery." The stranger looked confused and stared at Fiengus, who pretended to look at the map as knowingly as he could. "There seems to be a pattern here," he said, drawing the attention of the stranger away from himself and onto the map. "Look it makes a shape like something I've seen before, but I can't put a finger on it."

This caused the Mayor to leap to his feet, almost too enthusiastically. "Why isn't he just the man! I told you, I told you! Fiengus Longfinger is the very man for this. This is so much more than we have been able to work out. What do you think it could mean?" inquired the Mayor.

"Well, I'm not sure at this moment, but I think if I take it to my friend at the University, he may be able to shed some light on it," replied Fiengus, who was now desperate for an excuse to leave the office.

"Excellent, take it there at once. Let us know immediately what you find out," cried an excited, reassured looking Mayor.

"Then it's settled Fiengus, you will go to the University of Von Dufflestein and speak with this acquaintance of yours, find out all you can and then report back to us. We can then decide on the best course of action," said the stranger, holding out his hand to Fiengus. "Good luck and farewell Fiengus."

Fiengus took the man's hand and shook it, "Thank you and it's been a pleasure meeting you... I'm sorry I didn't catch your name."

"What you mean you forgot it?" said a perplexed looking Mayor.

"No, I'm sure it was never mentioned."

"I didn't think it necessary," the stranger said.

"Look I'm really sorry, we must have met before and my memory isn't serving me well. This is a stressful situation we seem to be in," said Fiengus.

"Do you mean to say you have no idea who this man is?" questioned the Mayor, who had a fresh look of uncertainty across his face.

"No, I feel I have met him before, but can't remember exactly when," muttered Fiengus, who was feeling a little embarrassed by this all.

"But, you must have read about him," said the Mayor "it was all mentioned in the pack we sent you."

"Pack?" queried Fiengus.

"Yes, the pack we sent you, it contained all the relevant information we have been able to gather on this mission. It was sent to you. I addressed the envelope myself," said the Mayor, looking to the stranger for reassurance.

"Yes, we did, it had everything," agreed the stranger.

"Sorry, but again no, I received your letter inviting me to come here this morning, and here I am, but no pack arrived," replied Fiengus.

"Oh dear," said the stranger, as the Mayor swept into another storm of wailing and uncontrolled dismay. "It appears that all of our information has been lost."

They were gathered, after both Fiengus and the stranger, who it transpired, was named Von Snare and who worked for the Mayor's office in the *Department of Strange Occurrences yet to be Named*, had brought the Mayor to his senses, around the receptionist's desk. It had also been revealed that this mislaid pack contained all the information the team under Von Snare had been able to gather, and due to budget constraints were unable to duplicate. The receptionist was bringing up all the recent mail and outgoings from the Mayor's office and had just traced the package on the list. "Here it is, and there's the letter that was sent, which was received by Fiengus," said the receptionist.

"Where was it sent?" cried the Mayor. The receptionist clicked on the package and checked for the details.

"It was sent to," read the receptionist, "well this can't be right."

"What is it?" inquired Von Snare.

"Well, this is the address that I sent the letter to and this is the address the package was sent to. They don't match up," said the receptionist.

"Eh, let me see that," snapped the Mayor. "Well how could that happen?" he asked.

"Well it says here that you filed this and sent it, Mayor," read Fiengus.

"Preposterous, I'm the Mayor, I make no mistakes. There must have been a mess up along the lines, let me see," and he grabbed the mouse from the receptionist and began clicking angrily on various icons. After some fruitless clicking the Mayor resigned that it was indeed a mistake and that whoever was to blame for it would be sought out and severely disciplined. No one pointed out that the Mayor himself was to blame. At this point he made a phone call to the *Department of Correction* and insisted that: "Someone be fired for this and it made well known what an incompetent they were and of course the press should be informed, but not of the leak of information, but only the incompetence and the quick rooting out of the problem." He ended the call by stating, "You know what must be done, and you're experienced experts at this, which is why I pay you on behalf of the good people of Von Dufflestein to ensure that they never know of such things. It's for theirs and our best interests."

After slamming the phone down the Mayor turned to Fiengus. "Right, it appears that the package has been mislaid, the details of which are unimportant, except for one thing, we know where it has been sent. This is a relief, and you are the man to collect it. As someone from outside this office, you'll attract little attention;

just making a call on an old friend, or something like that." The Mayor clicked on something, "I'm printing off the address. I'm sure I don't have to tell you to be discreet about this." He then reached over to the printer and thrust a sheet of paper with an address on it into Fiengus' hand. Fiengus was struck by how collected the Mayor suddenly seemed, a man who had, five minutes prior, been on the edge of a break down, now suddenly seemed to know exactly what to do.

"So you want me to retrieve this package now?" asked Fiengus.

"Yes of course, go there first thing tomorrow morning. You are partly to blame here after all, it was you who had the wrong address," answered the Mayor. "Just go to the address, explain that you think a package of minor importance has been wrongly delivered and state you would like it back."

"Offer, a small reward," offered Von Snare.

"Yes, people ask less questions when you pay them," agreed the Mayor. Fiengus looked down at the piece of paper in his hand and resigned himself to going along with this plan. The address was,

325 Metus Road

Von Dufflestein

VD314 JH6

Fiengus immediately knew this area. It was familiar to all, but rarely visited, and not by anyone he knew of. This was getting worse, but at least he had something to do, which seemed to quell his feeling of existential angst. However, this feeling was replaced by one of trepidation; the address was in the troll district.

3 THE TROLL DISTRICT

The following morning, several things were going through Fiengus' mind as he drove towards the address. Firstly, he was of course concerned about going to the troll quarter; it was not a place people went to. What made this worse was that he didn't really know why people didn't go to the troll quarter, leaving the reason open to his overactive imagination. Secondly, he did wonder several times what the diet of a troll might look like and if it bore any resemblance to him. To avoid thinking about the possible gruesome things that may or may not happen, he reflected on the day so far. To begin with, he liked having a purpose to his life, all be it a very uncertain one. Nevertheless, he enjoyed the feeling of being on a quest or adventure of sorts and decided that he would focus on that good feeling. This was of course accompanied by the fear of the unknown, but Fiengus felt that he barely knew himself, let alone the big wide world, so fear of the unknown should be ignored. The Mayor had crossed his mind too, and most of the thoughts of him were not flattering. Fiengus felt that it seemed unusual to have in charge of an important town like Von Dufflestein, a man so hopeless, so easily shifted in mood, to the point of instability, and as far as Fiengus could see someone completely useless at their job. His was a very important job after all.

He didn't have long to think about these things, as he had arrived at the troll quarter. After parking his car, he paused and looked up at the large gate that blocked the road ahead, which made up part of a very large wall. The wall could not be seen over, as it was so very tall and to add to its height and imposing character, forks and knives had been cemented along the top, all with their points skywards. Trolls, Fiengus recalled from an article he had read about them, were suspicious creatures. They feared most things and as a result were rarely seen outside of their own communities. They did not completely close their doors however, as they were afraid of not knowing what was happening in the outside world. From what Fiengus could gather, they were unpredictable and driven by a fear of most things, which made dealing with them very, very tricky.

Fiengus drew a deep breath and approached the gate. A large, brass horn stuck out of the wall with a smaller similar shaped horn underneath. Next to this sat a button and a sign that read: "Push the button and someone may answer, if not accept this and go away." This seemed a little rude and off putting, and with this and a wall crudely decorated with cutlery a bad feeling was finding home in his gut. He pushed the button. There was a few seconds pause. Nothing. He waited. Fiengus decided that he hadn't pushed the button long enough, and despite the sign, rang again. Again nothing happened. He became frustrated and was about to turn around and leave, when he remembered that he would have to return to the Mayor, who seemed to be incredibly severe on people who failed in their duty, even when it wasn't their fault. Fiengus resolved to ring one last time, and pushed the button down and held his finger on it.

A crackling sound came through the receiving horn and then a voice came through, "Stop pushing the button!" shrieked the voice. Perhaps it was the antiquated looking communications device, but the person on the other end had an incredibly high pitched voice. "What are you doing?" it continued.

"The sign said to push the button, so I did," replied Fiengus, who had by now removed his finger from the buzzer.

"Do you do everything that a sign says so literally?" Fiengus had no answer to this; the question seemed too ridiculous to bother with. The person on the other end continued, "What do you want here?"

"I want to enter the troll quarter."

"Business or pleasure?" queried the voice. Fiengus had to think about this, he remembered that this was a covert mission.

"I'm here visiting a friend of mine," he eventually answered.

"Are you visiting them for business or pleasure?" inquired the voice.

"Well," said Fiengus, "neither really, it's personal."

"You're being very guarded about this. Are they terrorists,

these friends of yours?"

"What?" cried Fiengus, "Of course they are not, what a stupid question."

"You think that security against the threat of terrorism is stupid?"

"No, but asking someone if they are a terrorist is. Who would actually say yes? Certainly not a terrorist anyway." Fiengus felt very proud of himself, for his display of irrefutable logic. This feeling lasted a very short time and was replaced by a feeling that he had said the wrong thing. This was doubly emphasised by the sudden sounding of a siren and a very large red light flashing overhead. Fiengus stood completely overwhelmed and was quickly surrounded by several, very large, trolls who grabbed a hold of him. As he began to protest, the troll to whom he had been speaking came out and said, in the same high pitched voice, "Take him, he's a self confessed terrorist."

"No I'm not!" pleaded Fiengus, who was now being led away.

"That's just what a terrorist would say," said the troll, smugly. Fiengus remembered how paranoid trolls were. This was not going to be easy to get out of. It took several calls to the Mayor's office to get Fiengus released and gain entry to the troll quarter. The covert mission was not going well.

He gazed for the first time at the interior of the troll quarter. What struck him immediately were the houses. They looked like ordinary houses; windows; doors; a roof and so on. However, what these houses had in abundance were security precautions, rivalling the devices of defence found in military bases. There were bars across everyone's windows, steel doors with intercom systems, signs that warned of death to trespassers and that large ferocious dogs lived in these houses, trained with the sole purpose of ripping apart anyone mad enough to venture too close to their owners or their property. The roofs were slick with a substance similar to Vaseline, and were topped with cutlery, pointing out at all angles as though attack could come from anywhere and needed defending against. There was a definite feeling of hostility towards anything that could be deemed hostile and as far as Fiengus gathered everything seemed to fit this category, including Fiengus, who was being eyed with suspicion by some trolls, from behind chainmail curtains.

Out in his garden, Fiengus noticed a troll, who had not noticed him, checking that his window bars were secure. Recalling his initial dealings with the trolls, he decided to try a different, softer tact. Speak less, be to the point and leave nothing to misinterpretation.

"Hello there," greeted Fiengus. The troll turned around and peered at him suspiciously. "I'm looking for a friend, but can't find his house, it's this address," he said as he showed the troll the address on the piece of paper. The troll gazed at it briefly, and then shot back into his house. "I've scared him away, I must have been too abrupt with him," thought Fiengus to himself. He was just turning away when the troll returned, but this time was brandishing a gun. Fiengus panicked and ran. As he ran up the road he heard the troll cry out, what sounded like, "Trespasser!" He stopped once he was out of sight and came to the realisation that this was going to be very difficult indeed.

Determined not to dally in the street and perhaps provoke some other unprovoked attack on his person he moved swiftly on. He eventually reached the address, keeping as low a profile as he could, which was difficult being the only human there who also happened to have an enormous finger. He knocked on the door and then taking a step a back, he looked up at the house. It was much the same as the other houses, adorned in the most outlandish security precautions he had ever seen. He thought about how absolutely terrified of the outside world these trolls must be and suddenly imagined them as being like hermit crabs, but only on dry land and without pincers and an ability to walk forwards and back and not just sideways... His train of thought was derailed by a voice that said, "I'm not in, I'm not expecting visitors and I'm not answering this door to a stranger with an even stranger finger!" The voice came through the intercom system, which Fiengus noticed had a camera that was pointing directly at him.

"I'm sorry, I'm looking for a package of mine that has been misdirected and posted here instead. It's from the Mayor's office to me you see," pleaded Fiengus, who was a little taken aback by the inhospitable nature of the troll's greeting.

"A package?" mused the troll, "I'm sorry but there's no package here, and even if there were why deliver it here rather than wherever you are from?"

"It was an accident, the Mayor... someone in the Mayor's office made a clerical error and sent it here," said Fiengus.

"What's in this package?" asked the troll.

"I'm not sure, but it's for me and it is very important," replied Fiengus.

"Why's it so important?" asked the troll.

"It contains top secret documentation about something I cannot tell you about."

"If it's so important why was it sent to the wrong address?" inquired the troll.

"As I said it was an accident. Look I really need this package, if you look on the package you will see that it has my name at the top," said Fiengus, who was now growing slightly impatient.

"Your name is at the top of the label on the package? So they got that right and the rest wrong?" asked the troll.

"Yes my name is on the top and this address is underneath it. My name is Fiengus Long..." said Fiengus, who was cut short by the troll.

"If the package were here as you seem to claim then why do you feel it necessary to tell me your name? Surely had it been written on there and if it were in my possession I would know what the name was. Now you are claiming to be the person whose name is written on the top, so telling me your name would be unnecessary as I should already know it," philosophised the troll.

"What? No, that doesn't follow. If you do have the package then yes you would know the name that was written on the label and yes if I were to claim to be the person to whom this package was originally destined then it would in fact need to be my name written on the package, but this does not imply that you should know that I know what the name is on the package, therefore me telling you my name and you then verifying this by reading what is written on the package, would thus prove that I am in fact the person to whom the package is rightfully destined," replied Fiengus, who felt very out of breath after such a long sentence.

"Ok, I accept that what you say is true, but you would need to prove that you are in fact the said person," responded the troll after a short pause.

"Look at my library card, that's my photo and my name there is Fiengus Longfinger."

"It could be a fake."

"I have a letter from the Mayor's office."

"They make mistakes, you said so yourself."

"Look I'm telling the truth, I am no liar."

"How do I know you are not a *liar* and you're making this whole thing up?" Fiengus noticed how quickly the troll had latched onto the word liar. He needed to be more careful with what he said.

"You are a pain in the... wait. If what I said about the Mayor's office was true then yes it could be a mistake and I'm not who this letter says I am, but if I were a liar then who's to say that I didn't lie about the Mayor's office, which would imply that the Mayor's office don't make mistakes and I would be who the letter said I was, but this would mean that there had been no original mistake and there would be no reason for me to be at your door, which is paradoxical; therefore I cannot be a liar and I'm telling the truth," said Fiengus, feeling that this must settle it.

"Maybe you're just inconsistent."

"Right, I've had enough, even if I was not Fiengus Longfinger, you certainly are not and as the name on top of the package is not your name you have no right to it," replied Fiengus.

"You're right, I have no right to the package," replied the troll. Fiengus felt that he was getting somewhere finally.

"So can I please have it then?" he asked sounding relieved.

"No," replied the troll.

"What?" Fiengus sounded somewhat taken aback.

"What you said was true and I realised this earlier, that I had no right to the package, so I took it back."

"Took it back, but where?"

"Where you return all mail, the Sorting Office," said the troll.

"Where is that? Oh god, this is too much," said Fiengus, who was feeling very down. He had to sit on the doorstep, he was feeling very sick. At this he actually began to sob. He felt terrible about it and very embarrassed. Through his high spec surveillance camera, the troll watched Fiengus and felt a pang of sadness at what he saw, which momentarily shifted his regular overriding feeling of fear. It was just enough for him to have a change of heart.

"Look, I'll show you, if it will get rid of you," replied the troll. Fiengus stood up from the doorstep, wiped his eyes and awaited the troll. He heard several bolts, chains, number punching and keys turning. The door finally opened and Fiengus looked at the troll for the first time.

4 AN INSTANCE

Don Von Jonn sat down in his study and put on his favourite record, it was an lp version of Queen's *Night at the Opera*. He leaned back in his chair and closed his eyes, the opening chords of Bohemian Rhapsody enveloped him in a warm and secure feeling and he felt the hairs on the back of his neck stand on end, in the same way they had the first time he heard the track. It was a wonderful and relaxing time. He had been working hard that day at the *Department of Correction* and had been successful in having three randomly selected employees at the Mayor's office fired with immediate effect. Relaxation was exactly what his wife had told him he needed after such a stressful day; it wasn't fair how they worked him so hard.

The fine, perceptible crackle, caused by dust created a unique effect to the listening of the song. These were the only imperfections that he allowed in his life. His was a life of order and everything only mattered in so far as others perceived it. This was evident in many aspects of his life; from his alphabetised album collection to the organisations of his shirts and ties to reflect the colour spectrum. These were only minor details and examples that did not reflect the extremes he went to for orderliness. At the other end were examples such as when he had the entire top floor of his house moved down slightly, to avoid having an odd number of stairs in the house. Only recently he had changed his car when he realised it clashed with a garden ornament. He simply could not tolerate the disorderly in his life and in fact revelled in eliminating it, especially when in the Mayor's office, where he was never in short supply of work. This was precisely why he was in charge of his department.

He mused about these things and about his perfect house, wife, children and life in general. It had always been this way and always would. Suddenly, he leaped from his chair and stopped the record player, just before the bit in the song where the electric guitar kicks in and everyone's heads begin to bob up and down uncontrollably. Don could not stand this part of the song, it made him anxious. Just as the music stopped the sound was replaced by the front doorbell ringing.

This was completely unexpected and so much so that Don looked at the record, thinking that the sound had come from it. The sound came undeniably through the house again and Don became flustered. "Who is doing that?" he grumbled as he gave his record a wipe with a cloth, returned it to the sleeve then replaced it in the alphabetised collection. After putting the record player back in the original packaging and then placing it in the music cupboard he made his way down stairs.

He cried out, "Just coming, you are most unexpected and you have not pre-booked this," he was checking his diary as he walked across the freshly ironed carpet, "so you'll have to wait," as the doorbell rang again. He looked at himself in the mirror and straightened his collar before turning to the door. He undid the latch, unlocked the bolt then opened the door. Before him stood someone he had not seen for a long time. "What are you here for? I thought you were..." he stumbled out.

"Dead?" said the man in a low husky voice.

"No, not dead, something worse," replied Don, who had gone very pale. "Look whatever it is you want, I'm very busy at the moment."

"You're still busy clearing up mistakes for that incompetent Mayor," said the man.

Don looked very anxious and whimpered, "Look, I'm sorry I have to go," he tried closing the door as he said this. "It was nice seeing you again." The man took hold of the door, stopping it from closing.

"I don't think so Don. You're coming with me I'm afraid, you see we need you."

"What for?" asked a trembling Don.

"We need you out of the way," said the man, smiling sinisterly.

"Please I have a perfect wife and children, please..." he pleaded. He heard a noise behind him. The man made a sudden movement towards Don.

"Who's that at the door Don? We weren't expecting anyone," said the voice of his wife. There was no answer; by the time she got to the door both Don and the caller were gone. She looked out, but saw nothing. She called out for her husband, but no response came. As she went to return to the house she noticed something on the mat. It was a small piece of paper, folded neatly in half. She took it inside with her. At the other end of the hall was a chair, which she sat down in, feeling suddenly dizzy. Once she regained herself she unfolded the note and read the message it contained. A frightful and sickening feeling rose in her stomach up to her mouth and she let out a stifled scream. Immediately she picked up the phone and dialled a number she had not called for some time. After three rings the phone was answered and all she said was, "There has been an *Instance,*" before dropping the phone.

She let slip the piece of paper, which unfurled on the floor in front of her. Once more she gazed at what was written on it, that terrible message of the fate of her beloved husband. It read:

Gone to Switzerland.

Love you all.

Don x

5 A PARANOID TROLL

Fiengus gazed at the troll, who was peeking around the door almost sheepishly. He had a large green head and bulbous eyes of an irregular shape, not round at all. He stood almost three feet taller than Fiengus and looked to be incredibly strong. But what struck him as strange was that despite his size and stature the troll seemed very, even by troll standards, timid. The troll was wearing a mask that looked like a strange piece of breathing apparatus that may have been an ancient piece of diving equipment. It was very crude looking with a mass of pipes sticking out. He eyed everything around him with utmost suspicion, giving the impression of a very poor actor trying to portray paranoia. It was all too much and when Fiengus offered his hand to shake the troll sprayed it with some strange chemical. "Oi," cried Fiengus, "I'm only being polite"

"It's for the germs, you might have anything," replied the troll, who then gave himself a quick blast from the canister.

"Is that what the face mask is for?" asked Fiengus.

"No and yes," said the troll. "Why do you want to know? Are you here to steal it?" he shrieked and retreated back to his house.

Fiengus realised that it was going to be very difficult to get the troll to come with him. "You know why I am here and you were going to help me."

"Oh yes," said the troll and he came back out of the house.

"My name is Fiengus," offered Fiengus, without putting out his hand this time.

"I know."

"Yes of course," said Fiengus, who looked expectantly at the troll, "and you are?"

"No I'm not, my name is not Fiengus," replied the troll. Fiengus could see that the he was not used to social interaction and had obviously misunderstood him. Either that or it was an attempt at a terrible joke. He asked him again, this time more directly.

"What is your name?"

"My name is Bogo Snot Troll," replied the troll, who then held out a hand limply towards Fiengus.

At this Fiengus smiled and said, "Nice to meet you Bogo," and went to shake his hand.

Bogo quickly withdrew his hand and screamed, "What's wrong with your finger! Is it diseased? You've got the plague haven't you? You have come here to give me the plague and destroy me!" wailed Bogo, who threw his arms dramatically into the air and looked like he might faint.

"No, it's just a long finger, it's not diseased, in fact it was a gift from the gods," said Fiengus, with a hint of pride.

"The gods gave you the gift of a long finger?" said Bogo, looking confused. "What for?"

Fiengus had never been asked this question by anyone before. People were generally content that it was a gift from the gods and that was enough, further elucidation seemed unnecessary. "I don't know, it was a gift from the gods, but I don't know why they gave me a long finger. It's a family trait, I think it used to mean something, but I'm not sure what it is anymore. I have been asking that question all my life," said Fiengus, who had a far off look people have when they are having a moment to themselves.

"I have heard of those who are given wings by the gods so they can fly, or super human strength, a great mind or fantastic courage..." he said as he momentarily paused on the word courage, but resumed, "but a long finger! What a pointless gift," he then proceeded to laugh out loud, rolling around on the ground.

"Alright," said Fiengus, with an expression of being hurt, "I get it, it's a bit useless really, but it is a gift from the gods though and that is special." He then looked at the troll and suddenly thought, "I like him", which was followed by the thought that he liked him because he had insulted him. This seemed strange, but he quickly forgot about it and said to Bogo, "I'm glad you're relaxing a bit now; let's go."

Bogo rose to his feet and stopped laughing, "Relaxing?" he said with a worried look on his face. "No I don't relax. That's when they get you," said Bogo, who then looked anxiously about him.

"Who gets you?" asked Fiengus.

Bogo looked at him with a worried look in his eyes and then said, "Maybe we should go. The sooner we get you to the Sorting Office the sooner I can get back to my house."

They then departed in what Fiengus hoped was the direction of the Sorting Office and hopefully the location of the package. He looked at the troll, who was avoiding stepping on the cracks in the pavement, as they walked along the road. He thought how strange he was, how he seemed so very frightened of everything. Fiengus couldn't imagine what that must be like; he got afraid sometimes, like everybody else, but to be terrified of almost everything he thought must be very hard. However, he recalled how he had grown to like him in the instance where he had insulted him. Another thing he had noticed was that he felt more relaxed around Bogo; Fiengus had been feeling very serious about everything lately. It felt good, Bogo seemed to make him laugh and that, he felt, was helping him forget himself a bit. He continued to think about why this was as they walked along the road.

6 A CUP OF CALMING CAMOMILE TEA

The Mayor sat opposite a distraught looking Mrs Von Jonn, feeling utterly uncomfortable about the situation. They were in his office, which was still in a state of complete disarray. It was morning now and the town was busily going about its everyday functions outside the Mayor's window. He offered a tissue, pathetically hoping that this might have some effect. "Would you like a cup of calming camomile tea?" he asked. "It always helps me."

Mrs Von Jonn looked at the Mayor and said, "Yes, that would be nice." The Mayor looked relieved at this momentary distraction and went to the door of his office and leaned out and asked his receptionist to fetch up some tea. He then sat down again in front of Mrs Von Jonn and was disappointed that she still looked distraught. He gave up on the thought of being an emotional support for her and decided he would get the facts about what had happened.

"So, Mrs Von Jonn..." he started.

"Oh, please don't be so formal," she muttered through her sobs. "Call me Hyacinth-Beaucoup-Tristan Von Jonn."

"Ok," said a slightly stunned Mayor, "can you tell me what happened last night; you said there was an *Instance*. You work for the Sorting Office?" asked the Mayor. Hyacinth-Beaucoup-Tristan Von Jonn nodded in confirmation. "The Sorting Office though, they should not have known about these... *Instances*. Tell me, how did you get to hear of them?"

"Well it happened the other day when a package came to us, it was returned by a troll, who claimed that the package was not his. He was very nervous and screamed twice during the conversation then ran off. This aroused suspicion with the person who received the package and they brought it to me. I decided that I should take it to our new boss," she said.

The Mayor moved uneasily forward in his chair and looked confused, "Your new boss, I wasn't aware that there was a new boss in the Sorting Office. What happened to Jones?" asked the Mayor.

"He quit unexpectedly, bought a boat and went sailing we heard, in Switzerland. Came into some money we thought. Strange he never had a leaving party, he loved a party, we just thought the new money had gone to his head and that he thought he was better than us."

"I never heard that... give me a minute." The Mayor went over to his desk and picked up the phone. He began speaking with someone and asking about Jones. He was talking in a low voice, as though he did not want to be heard, but actually drew more attention to himself as a result. Hyacinth could not help but eavesdrop. The Mayor was sounding more and more frantic, "How many more?" he asked. "This is getting too much and now..." he stopped and looked over at Hyacinth, who pretended not to be listening. The Mayor then resumed, "If people are going to be replaced in this office then I need to know," he paused, listening on the phone. "Yes I understand, but people are noticing... I have my man on it... Yes he is exactly what you wanted... Look I'll try to relax, but...he mentioned trying the University...Why? I don't know, he has a friend there he said...But I'm sure it's not him...What does that mean? That you can't take chances? Wait now listen..." He was cut short; whoever he had been talking with had obviously hung up.

The Mayor pretended to say good bye, then turned and smiled weakly at Hyacinth. He walked back over to her and began, "Some people huh? No respect for their superiors, just don't know their place. Not like your husband though, he knew how to do his job."

"Yes Don loved his job, said that he was never bored here, never a dull moment," she replied, before breaking out into tears once again. "Oh Don, what has happened," she wailed.

The Mayor shifted uncomfortably around, as though something hairy and with more legs than necessary was dancing under his shirt. "The tea!" he shouted, at which the receptionist appeared and offered out the tea. After drinking half her cup Hyacinth calmed down a little. "Ok, can you tell me what happened with this package," prompted the Mayor.

"Well I took it to the boss, whose name is Von Staninces," the Mayor scribbled notes and nodded to Hyacinth to continue. "He thanked me for the package and then asked me to open it up. I was hesitant at first, told him the story of the nervous troll and said he might have been a terrorist. He waved a hand and told me it was perfectly safe. I opened it and inside found some various pieces of information, photos and a map with a series of coloured dots on it, all relating to these *Instances*. That is where I got the notion my husband had been a victim, they all said they had gone to Switzerland. Why Switzerland?" she asked.

The Mayor leaped up out of his chair again, but this time with feeling and cried, "The name on the package, what did it say?"

"Oh that, it was a funny name, it was Fiengus Longfinger," she said.

The Mayor collapsed into his chair and his head dropped. "Is everything ok?" she asked. "Would you like some camomile tea?"

"The package, where is it now?" said the Mayor in a low voice.

"Why it's still in Von Staninces' office," replied Hyacinth.

The Mayor looked pale. He looked around the room as though searching for something invisible. He then turned to Hyacinth, leaped over the table and grabbed her, "We've got to warn Fiengus! He is in mortal danger!" he cried. He fled from his office, leaving a stunned and very confused Hyacinth-Beaucoup-Tristan Von Jonn alone. She looked around the room and remarked to herself how very different it was from her house, such a mess she thought. A good deal of time passed.

Something struck her; this Mayor was not the answer. She then decided to leave; she would try another avenue in finding her husband. The Mayor seemed too erratic and disorganised and too preoccupied with this package and Fiengus Longfinger, whoever he was. A silly name she felt. He was more of a hindrance than anything else. There was something about him that she didn't trust, something he wasn't telling her. His behaviour had certainly been odd. No he just wouldn't do, she needed someone more reliable and professional. She recalled the card her friend had given to her. She had said that should the Mayor turn out to be no use, try the number on the card.

As she left the office she saw the Mayor frantically shouting orders to a group that had assembled around him to find Fiengus and warn him of his imminent danger. "What is so important about that man? He doesn't seem to care so much for my husband who has worked for him for 15 years!" she thought to herself. She made her way out onto the street and entered a payphone. After entering the correct amount of change she dialled a number she had written on a business card. As the phone rang she read the card:

Alfitch Fiedson

Private Investigator Extraordinaire

"If I can't solve it then it ain't happening"

She thought the last line sounded odd, but she felt desperate. A voice spoke on the other end of the phone. "Yes, I'm calling about my husband, he's missing and I heard that you do this sort of thing, find them I mean not kidnap. You are like a sort of amateur sleuth, my friend said. Look I'm at my wits end and I can't think of anyone else to call," she said.

The voice on the other end of the phone said, in a strange accent she couldn't quite figure out, "That person is factually accurate, and you have just made the right choice. I am the best at what I do. Come by my office in an hour and we'll talk. Chow," the phone line went dead after this. The conversation was more abrupt than she had anticipated, but these mavericks worked in their own way. As she walked away from the phone box, in the direction of a milk bar, she imagined what he might be like, this Alfitch; he sounded intriguing.

Musings of a PI I

I was sitting in my office, with the light coming through the blinds in a way that reminded me of some crazies' personalities. I mused that I hadn't had a case in some time, but that my luck would change when the phone rang. The ring ring, ominous like footsteps on the roof at Christmas Eve; is it him or is someone stealing my tiles? I answered and this woman on the end says she needs my help, her old man's been snatched by some perps and I'm the man for the job. I tell her that I specialise in this kind of thing and she said she heard I was the best. I ain't one for bragging, but she was on to something there. So, I tell her to calm down, I'll do all I can to get him back. She told me I was a saint, but I said 'look lady I ain't no saint, I'm just a humble man with a gift from the gods.' Anyways, she was coming over in an hour and figured I should get myself together, have a shave, look presentable. Hey, I'm a professional after all.

7 THE SORTING OFFICE

Fiengus and Bogo had just arrived at the Sorting Office, which was back in the main part of the town, when Fiengus' phone rang. Bogo looked at Fiengus and asked, "Is that ABBA on your ring tone?"

"Yes Bogo," said Fiengus. "Do you like ABBA?"

"Of course!" cried Bogo. "I love ABBA. They are my favourite band ever." Bogo then began to sing the lyrics to the song and Fiengus then joined in. Soon they were laughing together. "Hey you're a great singer Fiengus."

"Thanks, you're pretty good too," replied Fiengus, feeling it strange that he had so suddenly begun to sing like this in public. He was also shocked that his paranoid troll companion had sung too. They continued singing, with a growing feeling of elation overwhelming them.

The phone stopped ringing. "Oh, that was fun," said Bogo. The phone began ringing again and immediately they began singing together. Bogo gave a good harmony, singing an octave higher than Fiengus. A small crowd gathered around them and began clapping in time, and then people started dancing, as though they had rehearsed it. It was a very strange sight, to see people suddenly break into what seemed to be, to the untrained eye at least, perfectly choreographed movements. This small corner of Von Dufflestein had momentarily transformed into Broadway. Eventually the phone stopped ringing and the singing stopped, the crowd then looked around slightly confused and dispersed. "People really like your singing Fiengus, you've a gift. I loved the way you did that sweeping pointing thing."

"You were great too, when you grabbed that woman in the crowd and danced with her that was brilliant!" remarked Fiengus.

"Who was calling, by the way?" asked Bogo, the look of universal terror returning again to his face.

"Oh, I'm not sure, I don't recognise the number. Probably not important anyway. Shall we go?" They then entered the Sorting Office, oblivious to the Mayor's frantic attempts to get hold of them.

The inside of the Sorting Office was similar to the inner workings of a bee hive. There was a frenetic energy everywhere, with people bustling around crying out to one another. There were pipes that sucked up letters and packages, sending them to unseen locations. Huge trolleys laden with mail were being wheeled from one end of the building to the other. The whole system of operations made no sense to Fiengus, it was too confused and random seeming. He had the impression that nobody knew exactly what they were meant to be doing, but were trying to make up for this by seeming incredibly busy.

"It's very warm in here," commented Fiengus. Bogo felt it too and was sweating more than usual. The source of the heat became apparent when Fiengus noticed a large furnace, which was visible through an open door. Mail was being flung into it by a large group of employees. Fiengus stopped a passing employee and asked, "What's happening to the mail?"

The employee stopped, looked into the room then answered, "Oh, that's just to make sure we keep our targets. That's just the mail we can't find the addresses of."

"That is a lot of mail to have been given addresses that don't exist," replied Bogo. Fiengus was trying to work out how much mail the Mayor sent out.

"No, no, the addresses probably do exist, we just can't find them. Some are really awkward to get to!" Both Fiengus and Bogo looked appalled.

"That's terrible, you can't just burn people's mail like that," cried out an indignant Fiengus.

"Well, technically we shouldn't but we'd never meet the targets set by the Mayor if we didn't. You should know that from working here."

"We don't actually work here," said Fiengus. The employee then straightened up, looking very stunned. She then swiftly shut the door.

"You probably shouldn't have seen that. Just forget everything I said." She then spun around and ran down the corridor. This caused Bogo to instinctively run too, hiding himself behind a large pot plant. Fiengus eventually coaxed him out and they resumed their errand.

"Very strange," commented Fiengus. Bogo nodded in agreement as they proceeded to the reception desk and rang the bell. A stern looking attendant came over and looked at them both.

"Yes?" he snapped.

"We're here about a lost package," replied Fiengus.

"Oh really, you have come to the Sorting Office for a lost package, how clever of you," sneered the attendant.

"I brought it back here, as it was wrongly delivered to my address," said Bogo. The attendant shot Bogo a hard gaze, which made Bogo step back and gasp.

"And now you want it back?" he inquired unnecessarily.

"Yes, the package is meant for me, my name is on the top," said Fiengus, who was getting a little irritated with the attendant.

"You'll have to fill in a form," said the attendant, with a look of officiousness.

"Ok, can we have the form then?" asked Fiengus. The attendant kneeled out of sight below the counter then reappeared with such suddenness that Bogo yelped with fright.

"Fill this in and hand it back to the attendant at the reception desk of the Sorting Office."

"That would be you then." The attendant looked confused and gave off the impression that he felt Fiengus was an idiot.

"Fill this in and hand it back to the attendant at the reception desk of the Sorting Office," he repeated in the same tone.

"Do you always refer to yourself that way?" asked Fiengus.

"What way?" asked the attendant.

"Never mind. Can I have the form please?" The attendant handed over the form. They began to walk over to a table, when Fiengus turned around and said, "Sorry, could you remind me again, what I do with this form?"

"Fill this in and hand it back to the attendant at the reception desk of the Sorting Office." At this Fiengus laughed to himself and then joined Bogo at the table.

The form was a maze of interrogative questions. Fiengus had to make several phone calls to fill in information that seemed irrelevant to anything. Where had he done his last shop; when he saw blue what did he think of; who did he think would win in a fight an eagle or a small group of hawks and so on in a seemingly endless string of pointless questions. After some considerable time the form was filled in and they returned to the desk. "There, that's it. So do we just wait for the package?" Fiengus asked the attendant.

"Yes, well done you've done your bit, you can just sit and wait now. Don't over exert yourself by doing anything in the meantime." Fiengus decided to ignore this. "You'll get your decision within 48hrs, once a commission is put together and they have evaluated your claim and validated your ownership of the package. You will get our answer in the post. Goodbye." The attendant then turned to leave, but Fiengus yelled at him.

"Hang on, that's absurd, we need the package now! It's of the utmost urgency!" The attendant turned and looked unimpressed. Fiengus was about to launch into another, more personal volley, when he remembered Von Snare's advice. "Ok, look that was a bit uncalled for from me, you obviously work hard and don't deserve this. You're just the front man, the cannon fodder to the general public; you are just doing what the fat cat bosses want. How about we get one up on them, eh? I could give you a little bonus," at which

Fiengus removed some coins from his pocket and winked at the attendant, "How about it?"

"Are you attempting to bribe an official of the government?" said the attendant with feigned horror.

"No, no, just looking to fund the process by which you can get my package to me that little bit quicker," insisted Fiengus, and not for the first time experiencing the feeling that he was not communicating himself well.

"I'll have to report this. According to the official rules, I am to destroy your application form with immediate effect and to end all dealings with you." The attendant then turned to a shredder and slowly and deliberately turned it on, seeming to enjoy and savour the moment.

"You rotten jobs worth!" yelled Fiengus. "Do you know who I am? Who my family is? Who my..." Just then a man in a suit, with slicked back hair entered. Fiengus collected himself, feeling a little ashamed of his outburst.

"What's going on here? What is all the commotion?" asked the man, looking angrily about.

"These two gentlemen were attempting to bribe me, they then threatened me, sir," replied the attendant with a sideways glance and smirk at Fiengus.

"Is that right? What are you two here for?" asked the man. Bogo was incredibly intimidated by this man and merely made a noise like air escaping from an inner tube.

"We came to collect a very important package that is in this office, it's mine and I want it back," answered Fiengus timidly. The man looked at the attendant, then held out his hand and took the form. He glanced down at it and his expression changed to a far friendlier one.

"Ah gentlemen, but of course you can have your package. Why I have it right in my office, I understand that it is of special importance and I took personal charge of it. Come this way." The man smiled and offered to shake their hands, which Bogo declined after making several attempts to do so. They then followed the man into the office and as he walked past the attendant, Bogo gave him a smile. The attendant was clearly furious, but said nothing. Fiengus laughed to himself as he entered the man's office, he had the feeling that things were going to work out well.

They sat at a desk across from the man who then introduced himself, "I am Von Staninces and I have recently taken charge of this office. Things were a bit of a mess here, shall we say. Too many people here were not taking things seriously enough. I was sent in to ensure that the machinations of this important institution were running as effectively as possible." He noticed that both Fiengus and Bogo looked a little bored so changed the subject. "Anyway, enough about me, you're here for your package," which he removed from a drawer in his desk, "and here it is. I must apologise, this has been opened. Not by me of course, by an employee, or should I say ex employee. I don't take kindly to those who do not respect other people's property." He then slid the package over to Fiengus, who looked at it briefly then back at Von Staninces.

"Thank you for this, it is a very important package... to me that is," said Fiengus. "Well Bogo shall we be off?" he said rising from his chair.

"Oh, just one more thing," said Von Staninces. "As a matter of protocol I need to know what you plan on doing with such an important package. For the records."

"Really? Is it important, because I'd rather not say; if it's all the same," replied Fiengus. Von Staninces expression changed slightly, to one more like he had originally greeted them with.

"Oh, it is important, I really *must* know. It's a matter of the utmost importance to me." He moved his hand back to the top drawer in a movement so slick it went unnoticed by Fiengus and Bogo.

"Really, well I can't say. Sorry."

"Ok, if you don't want to say, I can overlook this, in respect to your privacy and in compensation for the intrusion of your package." His expression became friendlier and he smiled at them both.

"Thanks, I really appreciate this, we're kind of on a special sort of errand, and I can't say too much though if you know what I mean," said Fiengus. Bogo nudged Fiengus from behind.

"I think we should go, I have a bad feeling about this guy," whispered Bogo to Fiengus. Fiengus felt it too; there was something unnatural about his manner, it seemed difficult for him to smile. Von Staninces, slipped his hand out of the drawer and concealed it and its contents behind his back. He stood up from his desk and moved around and stood in front of them.

"Well thanks, again we'll just be off then," said Fiengus. Von Staninces put out his hand, which Fiengus reluctantly took.

"A pleasure, Fiengus Longfinger," said Von Staninces. "Just one more question, if you would allow me the liberty."

"Sure, I guess," replied Fiengus, who really felt drawn towards the door.

"Who else knows you are here?" asked Von Staninces.

Fiengus and Bogo were both taken aback by the question. "I'm sorry, what did you say?" asked Fiengus, who tried to withdraw his hand, but Von Staninces tightened his grip and looked very serious now.

"Who else knows that you two are here?" he repeated.

Fiengus looked to Bogo, who had a terrified look on his face. Looking back at Von Staninces he said, "I don't see the relevance of that question. What do you mean by 'who else?' Who do you know that knows we are here?" He was very scared, but could not help but ask.

Von Staninces looked suddenly very angry, then smiled, but more naturally for him, more sardonically. "You are a clever one aren't you? Too smart for our purposes though!" and as he said this he began to bring his pistol, that he had concealed behind his back, out. However, before he could properly draw Fiengus' phone began to ring and Von Staninces dropped the pistol and put his hands over his ears, releasing Fiengus from his vice like grip. He appeared to be in great discomfort. "What is that noise!" he wailed, dropping to his knees.

"That," said Bogo, "is ABBA."

"Turn it off!" wailed Von Staninces, looking more in pain now.

"You don't like ABBA?" said Fiengus. "You know how it goes," and he and Bogo then proceeded to sing along to the ringtone. Von Staninces then rose from his knees, his face bright red in what looked like agony. His hands were held tightly over his ears and he was breathing heavily through his mouth. He stumbled backwards, bumping into the desk then made his way across the room, knocking over a lamp in the process. When he was at the other side he leaped through the window, which unfortunately for him was closed. The glass made a smashing sound that startled Bogo and Fiengus, bringing them out of their joyful ABBA fed stupor. They ran over to the window and carefully opened it. This was a little pointless, as no glass was left in the frame.

"I can't look!" cried Bogo. "I hate to see people lying on the ground, makes me think of dead people." Fiengus leant out the window and gazed down. It was four floors to the concrete car park below. Von Staninces was nowhere to be seen. All that was visible were the shards of glass that lay strewn across the ground.

"He's not there," said Fiengus, closing the window in rather a daze. He was shocked by what had just happened.

"Oh that's a relief," said Bogo, "actually no, that's worse. I hate it when bodies disappear like that." He began breathing heavily and had to sit down. "I need air, open a window."

"It is open, Bogo it's broken," said Fiengus. "Why do you think he did that? Very strange." Turning to Bogo, he asked, "What do you think he meant by me being too smart for their purposes?"

"I don't know, I don't want to think about it," said Bogo, before placing his head between his knees. "I feel faint, Fiengus. Open the window!" Fiengus decided to ignore him and went and collected the package, which was still on the desk. He was just about to look inside when his phone rang again. Bogo perked up immediately and began humming the tune with a big grin on his face. Fiengus was about to join in when he had a sudden thought. "Bogo, stop, I really think I should answer this call, someone must really want to get hold of me." Bogo looked disappointed. Fiengus answered the phone, "Hello?"

"Fiengus, why don't you answer your phone?" It was the Mayor's voice. "Anyway, I'm glad you're ok. I need to call an abort on the mission. You must return here immediately and whatever you do, do not go to the Sorting Office."

"We're already here," replied Fiengus.

"Oh god, get out quick!" shouted the Mayor. "There is a man there named Von Staninces, he is very dangerous, and we believe he is connected to these *Instances*."

"We met him; I'm in his office right now."

"Is he there?" The Mayor sounded frantic.

"No, he...he left very suddenly shall we say," said Fiengus glancing over to the broken window.

"And the package?"

"I have it here, its fine."

"My god, you're better than I thought! Brilliant Fiengus, get over here immediately. I'll fill you in when you get here," said a much relieved Mayor. Anxiety returned once more to his voice, "By the way Fiengus did you say *we* are in the office?"

"Yes, I did me and Bogo Snot Troll." Bogo waved to Fiengus, he looked much better now.

"Then bring him too, he knows too much. See you both

soon."

Fiengus looked over at Bogo and wondered how he was going to tell him this. Bogo smiled at him, but this quickly changed into screams and refusals as Fiengus informed him that he had to come with him. However, no matter how much he pleaded, cried and begged, Bogo Snot Troll was now a part of this, whether he liked it or not.

Musings of a PI II

So I met the dame like I said. She seemed down about her man being missing, but I managed to get her to see that I was the man to find him. 'Alfitch, I have the utmost faith in you to find my husband. Please, do all that you can.' I told her that I didn't fail at this kind of thing; nothing got me more hot under the collar than seeing a dame crying. I'd find those responsible and make them regret it, make them know that there is a wheel of justice and I'm the hamster turning it. The dame took my hand, looked me in the eye as though searching for my soul, and said 'You are a special man; I know that you will do it. Make them pay.' Like waves on the beach, hearing praise is still special to me, never loses its charm no matter how much I hear it. I felt that I had my calling now, my charge. I would find her old man, bring him back and reset the current to my tranquil ocean of justice.

8 A TELEPHONE CONVERSTAION

"Hello, it's me, Hyacinth. That guy you recommended, this Alfitch, I met with him."

"You did? What's he like?"

"What you don't know? You recommended him."

"A friend of a friend did, you sounded desperate."

"I am, the Mayor is useless and I want my husband back."

"I know it must be awful for you."

"It is, our perfect life is ruined. Anyway, I met this Alfitch and, well he's different I'll say. He spoke with this obviously fake accent, tried to sound like he was from New York or something, kept talking in really bad metaphors too. He was calling me dame too, who speaks like that?"

"Oh god, what else?"

"Well he seemed really confident about his abilities, and seemed to think that I was too."

"Why, did you give him the impression you were impressed, because you don't sound it."

"No, I remarked that his office was a mess and he told me that I was right, he had been busy. I also told him that I felt that his fee was astronomical, but he looked and said that I was right not to put a price on the best, then said something like you can have the hand crafted Italian leather shoes or you can have rubber plimsolls, then said I didn't look like I was here for gym class."

"He sounds a little unhinged, you didn't hire him did you?"

"I did."

"You what...?"

"Well I thought that these private detectives were, you know kind of out there guys and he was certainly that."

"No wonder he believes his own hype when, after all you just told me about him, you still hire him!"

"I know, but something strange happened after that."

"Even stranger?"

"I called him up, was going to tell him that I had reconsidered and to call him off, when he tells me he's got a lead in the case."

"He got a lead? Sounds like he's stringing you along."

"That's what I thought, but I'd given him a large cash advance, so I thought I'd investigate his claim."

"And what did you find out, that this Alfitch was an escaped lunatic? I'm sorry I even mentioned his name to you."

"No, he mentioned a name that I'd heard before."

"And?"

"Well I looked him up. I didn't have to go far, he works at the University."

"So, this Alfitch could have looked him up too; it proves nothing."

"That's not it; I looked through some of my husband's things and found a photo, with the guy from the University and Don with a group of people."

"Ok, you've got me interested, who is this guy?"

"His name is Professor Helmsman."

"Wow! He's famous! Well he used to be anyway."

"I know. And that's not all, the people in the photo, the others; I found their names on the back of the photo. Some of them corresponded to names I had seen elsewhere."

"Where? Tell me."

"They were on a list of names I had read that were inside the package that troll had returned to us, the one meant for Fiengus Longfinger."

"Ha ha, I remember that name, you told me. What a stupid name! Actually I have heard of them, the Longfinger's are a bunch of strange eccentrics that live outside the town."

"Well, these names on the list were the people who have been disappearing all over Von Dufflestein, the one's they're calling the *Instances*."

"Oh wow, this is huge! You have to talk to someone about this."

"I have. I have told Alfitch..."

"WHAT? You're kidding! You need to talk to someone who knows what they are doing, not this deluded Alfitch character."

"Look I know it seems crazy, but I have faith in him."

"I hope you know what you're doing."

"So do I. Well goodbye, I'll be in touch."

"Bye, and good luck."

Hyacinth put down the phone, looked across at the photo shopped family portrait, which constituted most of the wall above the fireplace, at her husband. "Oh Don, what a mess you've gotten into." A tear ran down the side of her face. She sat back on her Italian leather sofa and felt at a loss. Did she really trust her husband's well being to this Alfitch, a stranger and strange at that? She sat thinking for a moment then rose purposefully and declared aloud, "Something just doesn't add up." She left her house by the front door, got into her new, colour coordinated, car and drove in the direction of the town centre.

9 MORE TEA

Bogo had just finished his twelfth cup of calming camomile tea. He surveyed his surroundings. From what he had gathered, in the time since he had regained consciousness after fainting, he was in the Mayor's office; he was now involved in some mystery with this Fiengus and that now, because of this, his life was in danger. At the recollection of this last part Bogo let out a terrible, snotty scream and began crying.

"Good god, he's had enough camomile tea to take out a rhino. How can he still be like this?" asked a frantic Mayor.

"I am going to die! I knew it, I always knew it. I knew that there was something out there to get me, something in the dark awaiting me and here it is, it is YOU!" cried Bogo, pointing at Fiengus. "You will be the undoing of me! I should never have answered the door, opened it, went to the Sorting Office; I should never have met you, you harbinger of death. You are a curse, a curse..." he continued to wail like this for several more hours.

Once Bogo had settled a little and Fiengus having protested his ignorance of Bogo's fate, they then convened around the Mayor's most impressive and official looking table. Von Snare had joined them and was sitting at the right of the Mayor, who sat at the head of the table. "Right then," said the Mayor diplomatically, "we have established that someone in this room is, perhaps through no fault of their own, the cause of Bogo's impending doom... Fiengus. But, we can't dwell on this fact," Bogo regained his terrified look.

"The fact is," intervened Von Snare, "that we can avoid this by solving the case of these *Instances*. That means Bogo, you're safest option is to work with us, and logically you need to stick by the one who knows the most about these *Instances*, Fiengus."

"I wouldn't say I was an expert," said Fiengus.

"I agree, he's only an expert in the dark arts of sentencing the innocent to their untimely demise," interrupted Bogo, without looking at Fiengus.

"Oh, but look at you the expert at being a poor copy of a Shakespearean tragedy figure. What is with all this wailing and over-dramatisation of everything?" replied Fiengus, who was a little upset at being named a doom merchant and pedlar of extermination to the virtuous.

"What, a poor copy? We trolls take pride in our cowardice; it's what has kept us alive for so many years. 'It's survival of the yellowiest,' my father would say."

"'Survival of the yellowiest?' What rubbish, what sort of person encourages someone to be a coward?" retorted Fiengus.

"Look enough," interrupted Von Snare. "We need to work together on this one, whether we like it or not. As you can see from the notes, people are disappearing in a seemingly random way all over Von Dufflestein. If we aren't careful, people will begin to notice and that isn't good for the Mayor, and as representative of the people for the people this can't be good for them either. We need to act now and fast. Fiengus, you said before that you had a friend at the University."

Fiengus recalled saying this, but also remembered that he didn't really believe that it would lead anywhere, he had merely wanted an excuse to leave the Mayor's office. "Yes, my friend Professor Helmsman works there."

"You know Professor Helmsman?" said the Mayor, who looked momentarily distracted. "I didn't know that. What a coincidence."

"How is it a coincidence?" asked Von Snare, looking strangely at the Mayor.

"Well..." the Mayor paused and looked at each of the faces around him. "Nothing really... nothing that could help." Von Snare kept looking at the Mayor, suspiciously.

"Yes, I know him, but I'm not really sure how this will help," said Fiengus, returning to the subject.

"Look Fiengus, this is our only and strongest lead. You will need to try," said Von Snare authoritatively.

"Ok, I'll give it a try," said Fiengus reluctantly.

"Good man Fiengus. Once this is all over you'll get a medal and a public commendation!" cried the Mayor, leaping to his feet.

"Won't that draw the attention of the public, to something that we're trying to cover up?" said Von Snare.

"Oh, yes probably. Look, Fiengus, we'll be really grateful for this, but in a clandestine kind of way," said the Mayor, who looked over to Von Snare, who nodded approvingly. "Good, then it's settled, you'll go find this friend of yours and solve this thing once and for all," said the Mayor. He then looked gravely at them, still standing and implored, "Fiengus, you must not fail, I fear, so much is at stake, more than you know." As he said this, the Mayor walked over to his window and looked out. "I love this town, its people; I only do all this to best serve Von Dufflestein." Von Snare continued to eye him suspiciously, before accompanying Bogo and Fiengus to the door.

"The Mayor is right, this is very important. It's a lot to place on your shoulders too, and maybe this is not fair to ask. We have faith in you. It's funny, and I apologise for saying this, but I always thought that the Longfingers were disinterested in the affairs of others. But here you are willing to risk your life for the town. You're different Fiengus. Good luck." He watched them go, thinking some things through in his mind as he did. Once they were gone he turned and walked over to the Mayor. They had much to discuss.

"So, Mayor, what is *really* going on," he asked sternly. The Mayor's shoulders sunk and he turned from the window. He looked Von Snare briefly in the eye, and then looked down at the floor.

He sighed deeply before muttering, "I have made a mistake."

Musings of a PI III

I walked the streets, the darkness seemed fouler this night. My mind was occupied by even darker thoughts. Who was this Professor Helmsman and how was he mixed up in all this mess? What had he done with the dame's man? It occurred to me that he was involved, when I did some snooping around the Department of Corrections. I found a list of names, with the Professor's on it. All of them except the Professor were missing it turned out, mixed up in these Instances. Why was he the only one left? I had asked myself that question. Then it hit me, they were all working on some secret project, funded by the Mayor. Looked like something big, something worth a lot of money. Nothing can change a man so much as a few extra zeros on the end of a cheque. This professor was in some money problems, had a book out he'd invested a lot in, but it fell through. His angle it seemed: get rid of anyone else with a claim on the big pay out.

This all made me sick to the core. How could someone do such a thing? Well I'd find out, I'd ask him straight up what he'd done. I continued along the streets, it was all so clear, so black and white to me now. I was about to meet the devil in the flesh and look straight into his ink black soul.

10 THE UNIVERSITY

The University of Von Dufflestein was an ancient building. It had been around almost as long as the town itself. It had originally been a school of magic, but after a government inspection it was found to have a very flawed and ineffective curriculum. In all the years it operated as a school of magic, not one wizard, warlock, mage or sorcerer ever graduated. After the initial and unsuccessful attempt at teaching magic, the building became a university and taught, more effectively, a range of subjects, specialising in the sciences. As such, it was a revered place, but what actually occurred there the townsfolk were unaware. There were of course plenty of rumours, especially with regards of the department which Professor Helmsman worked in. It was a relatively new department and discipline and people were really unsure what it was all about. Nevertheless Professor Helmsman and several of his colleagues were famous worldwide.

The building loomed over them with its various towers, halls, dorms and so on. It had an irregularity created by the addition of new parts through the years; all reflecting the particular trend of architecture of their time and the various purposes and requirements the building began to have. Remnants of the Universities dubious beginnings remained. The domineering, gravity defying Wizards Tower, which now served as the ICT department, was by far the grandest part of the building. This contrasted with the more science orientated Observation Tower, a bastion of the progressive thinking of the time and meant as a statement of their movement away from the occultist past. It was constructed, after the building became a university, to make observations of the night sky more effective. As such the some 200 ft high tower was made exclusively of glass, which did allow more of the sky to be visible, than a traditional brick building, but no more so than if you had just gone outside. To remedy this, and the general feeling that it was all a bit of a joke, the dean of the time installed a giant telescope; the biggest in the world at the time. This of course made observations of the celestial bodies far easier, but placed immense strain on the glass superstructure of the tower. The very easily observed cracks that had formed meant that the very effective telescope was very rarely used, except in exceptional circumstances.

Throughout the interior of the University remains of its occultist past had become part of the everyday functioning. Cauldrons once used to brew supposedly magical potions, now served as hot tubs. The very large crystal Eye of the Necromancer served as a disco ball. Numerous scrolls and spell books kept tables from wobbling by propping up legs or held doors open. Even the wizards' gowns were used for the fresher's initiation rituals, which, in a nod to the Universities less than illustrious past, involved 'flying' on a broom over a swimming pool filled with treacle. This and much more, begged the question, what progress had really been made? It was a strange place aesthetically and in its workings. The staff themselves were well regarded as eccentric in the most polite of circles.

Bogo and Fiengus made their way through the great arch that was the main entrance to what was now the reception area of the University. A feeling and atmosphere of studious academia overwhelmed them and came through most poignantly in the portraits of former deans and lecturers that adorned the vast walls of the main hallway. Fiengus stopped for a moment to survey these and was going to mention something about one of them to Bogo, when he remembered that he wasn't talking to him; though Bogo did notice that one of the portraits, of a former dean, bore a resemblance to Fiengus. They moved on and made their way through the University.

As they walked through the building they were greeted by the smell of leather bound books, of oak wood, of freshly brewed coffee and an array of scents that stimulated the mind to thinking, this is a place where people learn. This was never clearer than when they entered the library. Though deserted of students, the room was electrically charged with possibility. On the vast rows of oak bookcases, there were books on every subject possible. Both Fiengus and Bogo were enlightened by it all.

As they made their way out of the library along the corridor they entered a large, open room with a huge staircase leading up to the department, where they hoped to find Professor Helmsman. Fiengus always hated this bit as it was a terribly steep set of stairs. They began to ascend. Halfway up they stopped suddenly, having heard a man's voice cry out. Looking up the stairs they saw an incredibly hairy man tumbling down the at great speed. He shot past Bogo and Fiengus, who raced back down to help. The hairy man crashed at the bottom into a janitor who was mopping the floor at the foot of the stairs. "You've ruined my experiment!" cried the hairy one, as he picked himself up off the floor.

The janitor shrugged his shoulders and then proceeded to act out feigned servility, "Sorry about that Professor, my fault absolutely."

"That's seven years of research down the drain. I shall have to start all over," he muttered; more to himself than anyone else.

"Are you alright?" asked Fiengus who had just got down the stair.

"Did you see what he did, this, this philistine, this hurdle to the advancement of scientific endeavour..." and he continued on in this way muttering to himself as he ascended the stairs until entering the door at the top.

"What a strange man," said Bogo, who was a little startled by the whole thing.

"Oh, that's nothing," said the janitor, "old Professor Nigel is only half as crazy as some of the others." He resumed his mopping and then turned to Fiengus and said, "You're here to see Professor Helmsman aren't you; I've seen you before, Fiengus isn't it?"

"Yes, and yes, right on both accounts. I've been here several times, but I've never met that one. Who was he?"

"That's Professor Nigel Hadambaker, he's been working on this theory of his for years now, spends most of his time falling out of trees, windows; tried to jump out of a plane once, before security stopped him," replied the janitor.

"Why does he do that?" asked Bogo, who shuddered at the thought of such activity.

"He's trying to disprove the theory of gravity. Claims that if he can just once show gravity to fail then he will have disproved it forever."

"The University funds this?" said Bogo, a little shocked. Bogo was anxious about the illegitimate use of funds and prodigal attitudes towards government monies and had written an erudite diatribe on the subject, but had been too afraid to publish it.

"No, but some crazy relative of his is super rich and has been funding him. I think it's more to keep him out of the way, so he can't embarrass the family."

"That's awful, no one should treat anyone like that," said Fiengus who seemed a little upset by this. They left the janitor and for the second time they ascended the stairs. At the top was a door that led to the department of Feesiks. Fiengus recalled how strange a place it was, but refrained from telling Bogo. He pushed open the door.

On the other side of the door lay another world, one that to the untrained eye seemed a mass of chaos and pandemonium. Once through the door it was necessary to take a giant, colourful slide down to the research floor of the department. At this level there were professors hard at work, which again to understand this as hard work you really had to know why the professors of Feesiks were doing what they were doing and to understand this was to understand what Feesiks was. It was all very complicated and Fiengus never ceased to find it mind blowing. For instance, four professors were currently engaged in experimenting with a bouncy castle, observing two of their colleagues bouncing and somersaulting, while precise measurements were being fed into a machine. In what seemed like a more conventional science experiment, two professors were adding various chemical to test tubes and beakers and heating them over a Bunsen burner. There was a big bang as the chemicals exploded. The professors just seemed to laugh. It would not be unfair to assume that they were merely blowing them up for the sake of it, but this would be to misunderstand Feesiks. While all this, and much more was going on, Bogo was in a daze. His eyes were lit up; he was in heaven.

"This place is fantastic," he declared as he danced along the piano key flooring, playing along to ELO's *All Over the World* as he went. Fiengus too began to lose himself in it all and began to walk dreamlike through the large room, mesmerised by flashing lights, novelty songs, fairground rides and the whole lot. So entranced he became that he soon forgot the seriousness of the work being conducted by the professors and even the serious nature of his being there. Laughing hysterically, he and Bogo made it to the other end of the room and exited through a door marked 'Seminar Room'.

Inside was a large room, with a great oval shaped table, made entirely from one piece of wood and surrounded by 24 seats, which were all a variety of lazy boys and bean bags. In various parts of the room were more professors, who were conducting all sorts of strange and wonderful experiments. One professor was using a dance mat and was measuring some unknown effect using a strange device. She was busily writing notes down into a journal and looking very serious about it all. Another two were in an isolation chamber playing ping pong. Each of them wore a strange device on their head, and seemed to be sending data to a computer, which was being watched by another professor.

They then found Professor Helmsman; he was in the middle of giving a talk in one of the small lecture theatres that adjoined the seminar room. Bogo and Fiengus sat down at the back and listened. On a white screen at the back was projected the title of the lecture, 'What is Feesiks?' Professor Helmsman had just begun and seemed very excited to be talking.

"Welcome to the introductory lecture on Feesiks. As I'm sure you are all very new to the subject, I shall begin with the beginnings of Feesiks itself, which is really the beginning of the universe!" he paused as though looking for a response, possibly laughter. When none came he resumed, "Prior to Feesiks had been the ancient discipline of Physics, which was quite good in its day at answering questions about gravity, which one of my colleagues is working on disproving at this very moment, the birth of star systems, black holes, the actual origins and workings of the universe and, well, quite a lot of stuff really. In fact it did this very well. But, it was lacking, and after the discovery of two new forces, that were shown to have more effect in the universe than anything else, it was shown to be inadequate at explaining these forces. And these forces were..." he then played a little pre-recorded drum roll, "the forces of Fun and Boredom. Duh duh duhhhhh!" He then paused again looking for a reaction, or to let the gravity of this revelation sink in. "Big stuff I know. Anyway, this meant that physics had had its day and that something was required to account for these two new forces and this was the birth of Feesiks. All the best bits of physics were kept, but were now reinterpreted from under the umbrella of these two new and opposed forces. This is really exciting stuff, really. I'll just give you a minute to talk about what you think this means and then I'll tell you." Professor Helmsman then proceeded to talk about the discoveries made through Feesiks research, such as the way music produced both effects, depending on its type; how the relativity of time, an idea from physics, was better explained with reference to the forces of Fun and Boredom, "Does anyone notice that when you are having fun time moves far quicker and when you're doing something boring time moves much slower." This continued for another 2 hours, until finally it seemed to be over.

"And so concludes my lecture on the origins of Feesiks." The crowd, those that were still awake, gave a pathetic clap then swiftly left. "If anyone has any questions you can email me, or get me on Twitter," he said with a slight hint of desperation.

The room quickly emptied leaving only Professor Helmsman, Fiengus and Bogo. Professor Helmsman was clearing up some notes when he looked up and then noticed his friend with Bogo. "Fiengus! How long have you been there?" he cried out.

"Oh, for most of the lecture, very...er interesting," said Fiengus unconvincingly.

"Really?" said Professor Helmsman with a look of disbelief. "Let's be honest Fiengus, it was terrible! The really exciting stuff, the areas of Feesiks that I've been researching, that's what I really want to be talking about."

"Well, why don't you, you might get higher attendance at your lectures." The lecture theatre had been very thinly populated by students.

"I can't though, the Mayor's office funds it and until it's complete we can't even mention it. I'm probably already in breach of our contract. By the way, who's your friend," asked Professor Helmsman, looking at Bogo.

"This is Bogo Snot Troll," said Fiengus and then quickly added as Professor Helmsman held out his hand, "Oh I wouldn't bother he's..." Fiengus stopped and was shocked to see Bogo shake hands with Professor Helmsman.

"Oh, it's such a pleasure to meet you. I've read all your books," said Bogo, whose eyes were lit up like a small child's when seeing their first Christmas present mountain.

"Really, wow, all of them?" asked Professor Helmsman. He was genuinely shocked, sales for his books hadn't really taken off. That was how his publisher had put it, only less politely.

"Yes, I really liked that one where you made the equation that proved that Fun could travel at the speed of light, as it had no mass," said Bogo who then went on to have a discussion about Feesiks, all of which went right over Fiengus' head.

"Ok, look if you two are finished we have pressing business to attend to. Look Professor Helmsman, I've been sent here by the Mayor to show you information he has gathered, regarding some strange occurrences; they've been named the *Instances*," interrupted Fiengus.

"The *Instances?* Never heard of them," replied Professor Helmsman. Fiengus then told him the story and all that they knew. Professor Helmsman looked over the papers, and paused over the map, "I recognise this pattern; it reminds me of something, though it seems incomplete." He then looked over the various photos. "Is there a list of names of those who disappeared?" he asked.

"Yes, this is it," said Fiengus handing over the list. Professor

Helmsman looked at the list then went white.

"Oh my big bang! Fiengus, this list, they are the team that I have been working with, on my research I told you I couldn't tell you about. A lot of them are from here, from the University. There are others, who I don't know, but most of them were on my team. I had received letters from them all, saying that they had all moved to Switzerland and wouldn't be back. I had thought it strange, but figured they had abandoned Feesiks for Physics, which is more popular there." He looked terrified, "This means that I am the only one left. Hang on a minute." He took the list of names and ran over to a desk and began searching for something frantically.

"Professor, what was the project you were working on?" asked an inquisitive Fiengus.

"All in good time, Fiengus," he replied, still frantically searching on his desk. Both Bogo and Fiengus were really anxious to know, their sense of curiosity was peaking.

"Oh come on tell us what it was," insisted Fiengus.

"Look I really shouldn't, we need to speak to the Mayor first. Now where is it?" he muttered to himself, throwing things around in a chaotic manner.

Bogo and Fiengus stood waiting for him, annoyed that Professor Helmsman would reveal nothing more. They were both completely unaware of the figure that had sneaked up behind them. The shadowy figure moved swiftly and struck first Bogo then Fiengus, knocking them unconscious. "Ah, I've found it, this is it, this is what I was looking for..." said Professor Helmsman who stopped when he noticed both Fiengus and Bogo unconscious. "Hey, what's going on?" he asked, not really expecting an answer and feeling a little silly for saying it out loud. A movement on his left caught his eyes and he just had time to catch a glimpse of a very short man, wearing a trench-coat which seemed to cover something large on his back. Before he could get a proper look he too was knocked unconscious.

The shadowy figure picked up Professor Helmsman, slung him over his shoulder and left, leaving both Bogo and Fiengus. On his way out he said to the unconscious professor, "Me and you got some talking to do bubba. There are some questions I have for you." He said all this with no sense of the absurdity of talking to a man whom he knew was completely unconscious. It was as though he was playing some part, but in a movie only he knew the script to. He left the University unnoticed, placed the unconscious Professor Helmsman on the passenger seat of his car, entered himself, then left.

BOGO'S DREAM

Floating through a field so vivid with colours yellow red blue yellow again with flowers and a soft breeze carrying the scent of spring bringing to the senses a feeling of rebirth and rejuvenation and and so much more such blissful feelings that one has when one is in total contentment skimming over the surface of a pond and look my face why it is a thoughtful handsome face the perfect green proportions and eyes that scream intelligence a frog and lilies white lilies everywhere dotted majestically across the tranquil pond a bridge but we need no bridge no we can fly and look that elephant has such long legs and its wristwatch is melting, what does it mean anything everything or is it time to buy a new watch who knows oh its my house and then I am but so young and so very different from now when is now oh it's gone but the young me is doing something no no no dont do it theres father hes looking upset no disappointed You'll bring shame on this family hes Fiengus now and hes pointing into the distance Im going in the direction he is pointing and there under a tree sits a man in a shroud and Professor Helmsman is there he looks and he smiles then he walks away leaving me and the strange man in the shroud listen, remember who you really are Bogo Snot Troll forget what you have become hes gone and Im in a small room with a table and on the table is a book with a pen beside it I open the book and find it blank I pick up the pen and begin to write it feels strange like something I havent done in a long time across the table sits a bull who is shaking his head and looks more angry the more I write but I keep on writing writing writing

Bogo awoke on the floor of the lecture theatre, his head hurt a great deal and he was very confused. He recalled that he had been speaking to Professor Helmsman when everything went blank. He also remembered his dream and the strange message. It was unusual for him to dream; it was normally nightmares that he had. He looked over to Fiengus who was still unconscious. Panic set in. What was he going to do? One thing came to him. He let out a huge, ear splitting scream that echoed through the whole university.

Musings of a PI IV

I had the goon who'd snatched the dame's old man. Had him tied up in a chair in a basement of an abandoned building. He was one tough guy, told me he knew nothing about what had happened, said he was a friend of her old man. The nerve. I gave him a slap, roughed him up a bit. He was like a jar that you couldn't open, but through the clear glass could see what you needed. Frustrating. He'd crack, all he needed was a little time, realise that there was no hope for him but me. He'd be begging me to listen to him soon enough. Patience, was all I needed.

11 HYACINTH INVESTIGATES

Hyacinth parked her car outside the government building, which housed the Mayor's office. She drew a deep breath, then exited the vehicle and made her way up the steps to the main doors of the building and entered. Inside she said, "Hello," to the receptionist, and then asked, "Is the Mayor in?"

The receptionist smiled and then said, "I'm sorry, he's in a meeting." Hyacinth knew that she would not be able to access the office now.

"Who is he in a meeting with?" she asked.

"Von Snare. He told me not to allow any visitors and to hold all his calls. It must be important." She leaned closer to Hyacinth and confided, "He's under a lot of stress at the moment, with all the work he has to do. Not to mention all the changes in management too."

"Changes in management?" asked Hyacinth, who was unable to hide the curiosity in her voice.

"Yes, lots of people high up have recently been replaced all very suddenly. I asked him about it, but he just told me that they were all off to Switzerland. I thought this was very strange; for so many managers to be going to Switzerland. They were replaced by outsiders too, not one of the jobs went to someone already employed here."

"Why do you think that was?" asked Hyacinth.

"Well it's all to do with the new work that they are doing here. He told me that they were here because of it. To help I guess; must be experts." The receptionist looked down the corridor before continuing, "There have been a lot of strange people here, all having meetings with the Mayor. At all hours too, coming and going." She moved even closer to her, "The strangest thing is how things have changed here so much since all this started, especially the way the Mayor is."

"What do you mean, by how the Mayor is?"

"Well, it's like he isn't in charge anymore. He's always been pretty incompetent at his job, between you and me, but he has never let that stop him. He always made sure people knew he was in charge. But now, with these new folk, he seems to be taking orders from them. It's like they are in charge."

"Wow, that's really unusual. I really would like to meet with him as soon as possible."

The receptionist checked something on her screen. "Well this meeting is unscheduled, so could end any time soon and he's free after this, which is unusual."

"Would it be ok if I just waited outside his office for him? Try and catch him once he finishes with Von Snare."

The receptionist thought about this for a moment then said, "Sure go ahead. I'll be right here if you need me."

Hyacinth thanked her then made her way down the corridor. Clearly the Mayor was up to something, but what it was she couldn't tell. As she rounded the corner to the passage the office was on she stopped suddenly, her heart missing a beat; someone was already there, outside the office and listening at the door. She recognised him immediately. The sinister grin was unmistakable; it was Von Staninces.

12 ONE OF OUR PROFESSORS IS MISSING

Fiengus awoke like a bolt of lightning had passed through him. He looked around himself, confusedly, wondering what the sound, which resembled the death cry of a fighter jet, was. "What's that noise? My brain has broken!" he cried.

"Oh, Fiengus you're alive!" said a much relieved Bogo, who had just finished screaming. "What are we to do? Professor Helmsman is gone." Fiengus looked around and agreed that he was gone.

"What's happened, all I remember is him looking on that table for something then I woke up on the floor," replied Fiengus rubbing the back of his head.

"Fiengus I had the strangest dream..." Bogo was interrupted by one of the professors entering the room. She came rushing over to them, very dramatically.

"What was that sound?" asked the professor.

"I screamed... Professor Helmsman is gone! He's been stolen! I got hit on the head, oh it hurts so much, and I need a doctor..." Bogo looked dizzy and sat down mumbling to himself about brain damage.

"Professor Helmsman is gone? Goodness, what happened?" Fiengus explained all they knew, which it was agreed wasn't a lot. "We should check the CCTV," suggested the professor.

They left the lecture hall and made their way to a small security room. They woke up the guard and asked him to play back the CCTV footage. They stared at the screen. What they saw left them shocked; they saw a short man wearing a trench coat who entered the lecture theatre and disappeared into shadow, he then appeared with such swiftness and fluidity in his movements that they had to slow down the footage. He struck both Fiengus and Bogo from behind at the same time, leaping incredibly high in the air to do so. The sight of this made Bogo faint. He then shot across the room and swept the legs from under Professor Helmsman, then after spinning around caught him under the chin and knocked him unconscious too. They saw him then sling him over his shoulder and leave the room as quickly as he entered it.

"Wow that guy's something else. He took care of you three pretty quick didn't he? He was really short too, like a child," said the guard.

"Well, he did attack us from behind," said Fiengus defensively, and then added, "He looks like a professional." He couldn't hide the fear in his voice. He knew that they would need to confront this stranger and after seeing the footage this was something that he really didn't want to do.

"What was with the huge back?" said Bogo who had just woken up, "he was like Quasi Modo."

"I've no idea, but is there any way we can find out where he went to?" Fiengus asked the guard.

"I could call my friend who works over in the *Department of Observation for your Protection*; he could watch the CCTV footage and tell us where they went. At least assuming this guy stays within the main town," replied the guard.

"Do it!" said Fiengus, and he did.

13 A MOMENT OF DANGER FOR HYACINTH

She couldn't believe what she was seeing; Von Staninces was listening at the Mayor's door. His face was badly cut, like he had been in an accident. He had the door slightly ajar and from behind the corner, which she was using to hide, she could vaguely make out the voice of the Mayor and what she took to be Von Snare. The Mayor was being told that he was an idiot, and he was apologising profusely it sounded like. This was strange, the Mayor never apologised for anything she could think of. She peeked around the corner to catch a glimpse of Von Staninces drawing a pistol from his pocket then entering the room. The voices in the room stopped and she then heard Von Staninces' voice.

"So what is all this? Have you forgotten our agreement? Well this will remind you," The sound of a gun being fired echoed through the corridor. Hyacinth held back a stifled scream. She looked around in panic for a place to hide. Across the corridor was a vacant office, which she slipped into. Peering out through a crack in the door she saw Von Staninces, who was limping badly, leaving with Von Snare. She could see the obvious fear on his face; Von Staninces was holding a gun to his back. Hyacinth waited till they passed then recalled the receptionist; she couldn't leave her.

She followed them down the corridor until they entered the reception room. Von Staninces was talking to the receptionist.

"I am terribly sorry," he said, very politely, "the Mayor has had a terrible accident. He has accidently shot himself in the arm with a gun. We've called an ambulance, but we really must go. If you could take care of him, I'm sure he'll be fine till they get here." He then smiled at the receptionist and turned to leave, "Come along Von Snare, we've an important meeting to attend." They then left, leaving a very shocked looking receptionist. She sat still for around a minute, Hyacinth watching her, unsure of what to do. As Hyacinth began to approach her, there came the sound of a siren from outside. Several paramedics entered the reception.

"Has that silly Mayor had himself another accident?" asked one of them. Before either of them could answer, they went down the corridor, as if it were rehearsed. Hyacinth followed them, leaving the still stunned receptionist. Hyacinth was about to tell them what had happened when she entered the office and found the Mayor sitting up and laughing weakly with the paramedics.

"Yes that's right," he was saying, "I accidently shot myself in the arm with this gun. I was trying to get rid of a pigeon that has been hanging around for days." They all laughed, except Hyacinth, who received a guilty look from the Mayor, who then asked to be taken away. She followed him to the ambulance.

"What's going on Mayor?" she asked. The Mayor looked nervously at her.

"I told you, it was an accident," he pleaded.

"Look, unless you are family you can't come," said one of the paramedics, shutting the door to the ambulance. Hyacinth watched them pull away and disappear around a corner. Something far worse than she could ever have imagined was happening. She needed help; it was clearly too dangerous now. She took out her phone and made a call.

14 THE INTEROGATION

Professor Helmsman awoke with a pain in his head and struggled to focus on his surroundings, having had the contents of a bucket of water thrown over him. Coughing and spluttering and feeling his heart race, he made to move, but found himself tied to a chair. "Hello?" he asked, really hoping not to receive an answer. When none came he looked around taking in the room he was in. It was low ceilinged, with some light coming in from a small window high up, giving the impression that he was underground. "A cellar perhaps?" he thought to himself. The room had a dank smell that added to the subterranean impression; it felt disused, like no one had been here for some time. Something moved in the corner and before Professor Helmsman could say anything an incredibly bright light suddenly flooded the room, so bright as to make it impossible to see. Through his squinted eyes he made out a shadowy figure moving towards him.

"Tell me about these *Instances* and about the man Don and you might get out of this a fraction of the man you are now," came a gruff, threatening voice. Professor Helmsman looked at the figure descending upon him, fear gripping him and a need to know one thing came upon him.

"What fraction exactly?" he asked.

"What?" replied the confused though still threatening voice, "Just a fraction."

"I need to know though; I mean even a rough estimate."

"Are you testing me?" replied the man, looking confused and angry in equal measures.

"No, I just deal in facts and can't stand uncertainties. Plus I'm not sure I really want to be just half a man. And then there's the question of which half. No I need to know." The figure stopped then looked around.

"This isn't how this thing works, you just answer my questions. You don't ask the questions, I do," at this the figure then threw another bucket of water over Professor Helmsman.

"Oh, why do that?" asked Professor Helmsman. The figure responded by launching forward and hitting him in the head with the bucket. "Ouch," he cried.

"I ask the questions bubba, not you!" cried the figure. "Now tell me where Don is and what you know about these *Instances!*" Professor Helmsman swallowed hard as the stranger drew nearer.

Meanwhile, Fiengus and Bogo had been informed of the location of Professor Helmsman. They had raced round in Fiengus' car and stopped across the street. He was last seen on the CCTV footage entering a small warehouse and they were now outside.

"Wow, this is so..." Fiengus said, "Oh, what's the word?"

"I don't know, give me a context," offered Bogo.

"Ok. Eh, let me see. Well it's like this building, an abandoned warehouse, the trench coat the guy was wearing; you know taking a prisoner here. I mean that he probably has him in a basement inside."

"A cliché?" ventured Bogo.

"Yeah that's it!" said Fiengus.

"It is isn't it! Imagine if he has tied Professor Helmsman to a chair and he's shining a light doing the whole tough guy act!" Both Fiengus and Bogo started laughing.

"And I bet he threw a bucket of water on him to wake him up too!"

"Stop," laughed Bogo. Fiengus looked at him and then smiled.

"Hey Bogo I'm glad we're talking again. Look I'm sorry to have got you into all of this, I know that you're afraid of everything and this must be very hard, what with the kidnappings and disappearances and narrowly avoiding being killed by that Von Staninces..."

"Ok, ok, I accept your apology. Let's not talk about our predicament though, it makes me have butterflies in my stomach and I'm really scared of butterflies," replied Bogo, who looked a little pale and was sweating a lot. "And I'm sorry too. You're like a real friend to me, Fiengus and although this may lead to my eventual death or worse, I'm glad that your mail was misdirected to my house," as he said this, Bogo had to turn away, and Fiengus was sure that he caught a glimpse of a tear in his eye.

"Wow, Bogo did you mean what you just said?"

"About being glad to have met you?"

"No, about being scared of butterflies?"

"Yes, it's a condition...hey stop laughing!" said Bogo, but Fiengus was laughing very hard and had to lean against a wall to catch his breath. It took a minute for Fiengus to compose himself.

"Ok, let's go get the Professor," he said in a determined sort of way that Bogo had not heard him use.

They were now round the back of the building, and could vaguely make out the sound of voices coming through a small window at ground level. Fiengus looked in and could make out Professor Helmsman in a chair and someone else was in there with him.

"Oh my god!" said Fiengus.

"What, is he dead? Is he torturing him?" asked Bogo, looking like he might come down with another panic attack.

"No, he's tied him to a chair in the basement and is shining a really bright light at him, the guys even wearing a trilby now!" laughed Fiengus. Bogo began snorting and laughing too.

"Stop, stop! This guy is hilarious. It's a shame he didn't have a friend, they could have done the good cop, bad cop thing!" said Bogo.

"That would be brilliant," replied Fiengus. "Hey, we should

listen to what they are saying." Fiengus could hear Professor Helmsman telling the man that he had been working with someone called Don and that they had been working on a top secret project.

"That must be the one that he told us about; the one he said he couldn't tell us about! I hate when people do that, get you all excited and then do that 'oh I can't tell you, I've said too much,'" said Bogo.

"Yeah, I really want to know what it is. I don't think he'd tell us, but this guy's been beating and torturing him; it even looks like he's thrown water over him too!" Bogo sniggered at this, "He's bound to tell him."

"We should listen to what he has to say and then you can burst in and rescue him once he tells his secret," suggested Bogo.

"I should burst in and rescue him?" asked Fiengus looking surprised.

"There's no way I'm going in there! I'm afraid of butterflies, remember," reasoned Bogo.

"True, ok we'll listen to what he has to say then I'll burst in, take the little guy by surprise then rescue Professor Helmsman. And if it's too late and he kills him then really it's Professor Helmsman's fault for not telling us, and teasing us with half a story."

"Yeah, it is his fault; we're doing what's right. Ok, what's he saying?"

Fiengus leaned up to the window and listened carefully. He made out the voice of Professor Helmsman. "And that's the secret project we were working on, that's absolutely everything I know about it and now you know."

He then heard a phone ringing and the man's voice on the phone, "What, are you sure?

"Damn! Too late! Right I'm going in," and then Fiengus dashed courageously through a door, into the basement. He felt more alive in that moment than at any other time in his life, like a lion on the savannah plains leaping at its prey; like the salmon making it to the top of the falls. He could feel the blood pulsing through his veins and he actually roared out loud. He imagined himself rushing into the room, tackling the man to the ground then running over to Professor Helmsman, but he was different, he was a beautiful lady, who was smiling at him...

Inside the room this feeling faded very quickly and was replaced quickly by one of self consciousness and the reality that he had no plan and no next move, which all struck him like a bucket of water. He froze. "Fiengus is that you?" asked Professor Helmsman his face looking almost embarrassed, "Did you just roar?"

Fiengus felt incredibly out of his depth, but had sense to ignore Professor Helmsman's last question. "Yes it's me and you there, if you don't unhand this prisoner then I'll..." stuttered Fiengus.

"What?" the man asked. He looked distracted and was putting his phone away into his pocket. Fiengus mistook this for him going for a gun and suddenly foresaw the end of his short life. He had started out on this journey to find himself and now he was going to die. It was all going so horribly wrong and so quickly. He started crying and screamed, "No please don't..." just then a shadow leaped into the room and tackled the man. They struggled on the floor, and then a sound like a sharp crack filled the room. They stopped struggling then the man stood up, looking stunned, and dashed out of the door.

Fiengus stood and then checked his trousers; dry. He then rushed to Bogo. "Bogo, Bogo, are you alright?" he cried.

"Yes, I think so," he said. Fiengus looked at him and saw his face had changed, he looked completely different, the fear in his eyes was gone, replaced by something he felt he may have seen before, but was not confident enough about it to mention at the time.

"Bogo, you saved my life there, you...you were incredibly brave!" Fiengus said with a look of astonishment. "But, I thought you were afraid of everything?" asked Fiengus. Bogo looked at him, then sighed and shrugged his shoulder, indicating that he was about to tell him something he hadn't told anyone before.

"The truth is Fiengus, I'm not really a coward. In fact, I'm completely reckless and fearless and I mean of truly heroic stature," confided Bogo, with a look of sadness.

"But, that's brilliant Bogo, that's absolutely brilliant!" Fiengus said excitedly and he rose to his feet.

"You don't understand, Fiengus, only a troll can. We pride ourselves in our cowardice, it's what has kept us alive for so many years. My family especially, they were highly respected cowards and then I came along. I'd go out at night, without a care and climb trees blindfolded. I once juggled lit dynamite and narrowly avoided blowing myself up. I sought out danger wherever I could find it but it was never enough. Then one day my father sat me down and said, 'Son, you have brought shame on this family with your acts of bravery. It's not our way'. At first I laughed and then jumped out of our third floor window and rode my horse backwards along the cliffs for a bit. But the seed was planted and slowly I began to feel terrible and eventually vowed to my family that I would do all I could to overcome my bravery and try to be a coward. I tried very hard, but couldn't do it for a long time. I would get it all wrong, get scared inappropriately or miss really good opportunities to scream or soil myself. Eventually I came to the conclusion that I was going to need to get drastic in my efforts and that's when I started to pretend to be afraid of everything, it was the only way that I could appear normal. My family were very proud at first, having the most terrified troll within their midst was something of a reason to hold their heads high. But it got too much and I eventually locked myself away from the outside world; the act had exhausted me. I never set foot outside my door for 2 years and then, then your package came Fiengus and I knew it was a sign. I returned it to the *Sorting Office* knowing that if you came for it then I would have to take you there to retrieve it; they have such an incredibly complicated application process for the return of mail that there was no way they would give it to you without me being there. I saw this as my excuse to return, but I was terrified, genuinely terrified. All those years hidden away had done something; they had made me afraid; it was no longer an act. But then this happened," said Bogo, looking suddenly worried again, "You can't say anything about this, for my family's sake, it would destroy them to think that I was returning to my reckless ways." The familiar look of terror was beginning to return to Bogo's face.

"I won't say anything Bogo," said Fiengus, who put a hand on Bogo's shoulder and opened his mouth to say something when from a corner of the room came a sound.

"Look this is lovely, but could someone please untie me!" cried out Professor Helmsman.

After releasing Professor Helmsman from his bonds and making up several excuses as to why there was such a delay in coming to his rescue they decided they needed to go somewhere quiet and where no one would be. They decided on the University Library and were now sat around a table with coffees in disposable cups discussing what they now knew and what they were going to do next. Professor Helmsman was telling them about the top secret project he had been working on and did so in great detail, explaining how the team was put together. It was a far longer speech than Bogo had taken to explain his entire life. It was his way; he liked to talk about stuff, a lot.

"Ok, let me sum up what you've said," said Fiengus. "You were working on a top secret project, funded by the Mayor, to research the opposing forces of Fun and Boredom, in what you call the Opposition Theory. So basically Feesiks research, but this was bigger. This involved a threat to life in Von Dufflestein, something had been sighted in space that was moving towards earth and was centred on this town. Why this town?"

"We couldn't work out why, but this intense force of Boredom was coming this way. It had something to do with a discovery we made, the most powerful medium for the force of Fun," answered Professor Helmsman.

"And that was the thing you discovered in the book?" asked Bogo.

"Yes, but it wasn't a science book, but a strange religious book. The book was discovered here in Von Dufflestein and was brought to us. It talked about the beginnings of the universe, about how the Spectral Beings had created the universe and in doing so created the two forces of Fun and Boredom."

"Wow, that's a real coincidence," remarked Fiengus.

"That's exactly what we thought, here we were making these grand discoveries in what we thought was ground breaking stuff, strictly in the realms of pure science, and a lot of what we were finding was in this strange little book. But that wasn't the biggest coincidence. We'd been researching ancient methods for producing Fun, to see if there was anything of worth out there. This included racing around on ostriches, train spotting, collecting stamps and even watching people just going about their everyday lives on TV. They were all bizarre and had little observable traces of Fun, but often high on the Boredom scale. However, we came across a now outdated form of entertainment, it was big in the 1980s and had some success in several parts of Asia, but was pretty much an antiquated practice," continued Professor Helmsman.

"And this is what you found mentioned in the book?" asked Bogo.

"Exactly, the book opened with the line, 'In the beginning was the sound and the sound was Karaoke'," said Professor Helmsman solemnly. There was a short silence around the table.

"I've heard of it. Didn't it involve people meeting in houses, clubs and so on and then singing along to popular songs, usually badly and inaccurately?" said Fiengus.

"That's what we thought, but when we ran tests on it the results were, well phenomenal. We tested it on concentrated samples of Boredom and it almost completely eradicated them. It just seemed to be missing something. We have tried working on adding some dancing and this had some effect, but something seemed to be missing and this is where our research ended. The Mayor pulled the plug on it, said due to unforeseen errors made somewhere in the government the budget was no longer available for us and that was it. We tried continuing on; pulling resources from independents, but still haven't been able to find the missing element. I brought the results of our research to the University, to keep it safe. I haven't seen any of the members of our team since. Then you tell me that they have all been disappearing. It really was such important discoveries we were making"

"It doesn't make any sense that the Mayor pulled the funding like that. You said that this research was started because of something that was seen to be coming this way," said Fiengus looking perplexed.

"A terrible threat to life on earth!" stated Bogo, looking nervously upwards.

"That's what we thought. It was so sudden too; we were one minute measuring the observable effects on a quantum level of House of Pain's *Jump Around*, when the Mayor comes in and tells us that the work in no longer deemed important and that the funding is no longer available," replied Professor Helmsman, looking rather upset. "We really were on to something; you should have seen the results."

"You said that it affected people too," asked Bogo.

"Yes, people would sometimes begin to dance, hum, sing along etc, when certain songs were sung," replied Professor Helmsman.

"That's weird, when Fiengus and I were singing along to his ring tone people began to do exactly that," said Bogo, looking back at the group.

"Yes, they did and when we were in Von Staninces office we started singing and he seemed really distressed by it all, even threw himself out of his window," added Fiengus. Bogo shuddered at the mention of this.

"Really?" asked Professor Helmsman, looking very interested. "Tell me, this Von Staninces is somehow linked to these *Instances* and when you sang he had to flee. What exactly were you singing?"

"ABBA," both Fiengus and Bogo said at the same time.

"ABBA?" asked Professor Helmsman almost to himself. "Wait one second," and he drew a notebook from his pocket and began scribbling something down. He leaped from his chair and cried out

"That's it! That's the final piece of the equation! He jumped around excitedly, like a small boy who just got a puppy. Both Bogo and Fiengus stared at him, unsure of how to act. He leaned over the table towards them and exclaimed excitedly, "We have to return to the Feesiks department immediately, we need to show you the Machine. This could be it gentlemen, this could be the greatest discovery ever made!" He was beaming across his face.

"Hang on, we need to go to the Feesiks department, why?" asked Fiengus, still looking very confused.

"Why?" asked Professor Helmsman rhetorically, "To save the world that is why!"

Musings of a PI V

The darkness of the streets, as I walked them alone, seemed to mock me. Even the rain seemed to understand it was better than me. How could I be so wrong? All the evidence seemed to point to the Professor being involved in this, but not how he described it. Strange science, experiments and secret projects funded by the Mayor. This threat to us all. Then the phone call from the dame, telling me that the Mayor and someone call Von Staninces are involved. It's too much for a guy like me to deal with. Maybe the old me could have done something, but he isn't coming back, he can't, can he?

The neon lights of a bar beckon me now; call out like a siren to a lost ship with sweet intonations, but leading ultimately to destruction. What do I care? Sit down at the bar, order my drink, and look up at the TV. An old movie is playing, I recognise it. A detective is pursuing this precious statue of a bird, which is disguised to look valueless, but is actually covered in precious stones. In the end it is a fake. Staring at this I get to thinking about my own predicament, I thought I was pursuing the truth, but I found I was wrong. Do I just quit? No, I find my real culprit behind all of this.

Ah, what am I saying? I'm being unrealistic. I down my drink put on my hat and toss the bartender what I owe him. I have a sudden feeling deep down in my gut that things are going to change, in a big way. I need to get to my office and call the dame, find out what she knows. I need to tell her I quit. This ain't my line of work no more.

15 BEARDS AND PLANS

They were gathered back at the department of Feesiks and a very excitable Professor Helmsman was talking erratically and bouncing about. Several other professors were there listening and talking amongst themselves. Many beards were rubbed and many "ahs" uttered in that room, that day. Amongst the hustle and bustle of it all sat Fiengus and Bogo, feeling a little out of their depth. From what they could gather the plan was:

1. Run final checks on the Machine and gather together as many ABBA albums as possible
2. Attach Professor Beeswax's prototype dance mat to the Machine
3. Discover the meaning of the strange pattern that seemed familiar on the map, which indicated the locations of the *Instances*
4. Figure out how to stop the *Instances*
5. Have lunch
6. Find the Monk

The final item on their to-do-list intrigued them the most. They had never heard of the Monk, and asked Professor Helmsman who he was.

"The Monk, is a member of an ancient order, the ones that wrote the book I was telling you about that referenced Karaoke," said Professor Helmsman.

"What is this book called by the way?" asked Bogo.

"The book is called *The Story of Life*," answered Professor Helmsman.

"That's a rubbish name," said Fiengus, who suddenly felt like someone living in a glass house operating a crane with a wrecking ball. "Anyway, why is he called the Monk? Why not just Monk? Is he someone special?"

"That's what we thought, we figured he was some very revered member of their sect and that was why he was called the Monk, but it turns out it's because he's the only one. Which is less grand," stated Professor Helmsman.

"He's the last one?" asked Bogo. "What happened to them all? Plague? Famine? Pestilence? Barbarians? The Inquisition?"

"No Bogo, none of these," interrupted a Professor, who went by the name Kinootz. "They just seem to have disappeared," he continued, attracting the attention of everyone there. He had a voice that demanded attention, like David Attenborough. "It all happened a long time ago. Their sect went round the world training people in the art of Karaoke, in the hope that they could stem the tremendous power of Boredom, which was more prevalent back then, with there being no TV, internet and so on."

"What did people do?" asked one of the younger Professors.

"Oh they were far more aggressive. Wars were waged, people were horrible to each other and all because they were so utterly bored," resumed Professor Kinootz, who paused briefly to wipe his glasses. Fiengus leaned over to Professor Helmsman and asked who Kinootz was.

"He's a Professor of Feesiks primarily, but he has used the new found knowledge to reinterpret historical events. From his perspective and research, which has won him the Nobel Prize, he showed that many of the abominations of human nature could be attributed to Boredom. He showed, for example, that Genghis Kahn, Hitler, Stalin and many other horrific characters from history all suffered from what is now called Chronic Boredom. This means that, in the same way radiation can have very adverse effects on the human body, the force of Boredom can have effects too. One such effect being, in extreme cases, warmongering," whispered Professor Helmsman. "These intense locales of Boredom are referred to as Boredom Singularities. It's just a theory at the moment, but is generally accepted in most academic circles." Fiengus sat back taking this all in. It seemed to make sense to him, but it was still a lot to digest in one go. Professor Kinootz then continued.

"So, this was the role that the sect, called the Order of Eudemonia, took upon themselves. They decided that it was their duty to combat the power of Boredom and did so using Karaoke, which is mentioned in their book. You see, according to their belief, when the universe materialised the first thing created was the sound of Karaoke. After this everything began to unfold and come into being as the wave of this sound travelled through nothingness, expanding the universe as it went, and still does. It is theorised that if one could travel faster than the speed of light, an impossibility shown by Physics, then you would be able to catch up with this sound and hear the ethereal, mellifluous initial melody of the universe. Ah, to be able to do such a thing. Anyway, enough daydreaming. This sect did very good work, averted many crises that could have spelled the end of humanity, or so it is told. However, they began to lose their reason to be when mankind started creating other means of Fun. They became almost obsolete, as there really seemed to be no real need for such powerful modes of Fun, when the force of Boredom was as weak as it was."

"Hang on a minute," said Fiengus, "Isn't Karaoke a form of entertainment that mimics already established pop songs?"

"That is correct," said an impressed looking Professor Kinootz.

"Well how could the first thing in the universe be something that is a copy of something else? It's like an echo, it needs an original caller, or ripples in a pond need a stone to be dropped," said Fiengus.

"Well that seems like a paradox, doesn't it and you raise a great theological question there. The answer is that the Karaoke that came into being in the universe, the physical universe that is, is a copy of a Karaoke which exists in the realm of the Spectral Beings, which is itself a copy of the original music of their realm."

"So it's a copy of a copy?" asked Fiengus.

"Yes," confirmed Professor Kinootz, looking thoroughly impressed with Fiengus, who was himself feeling that he was finally getting all this, that it wasn't over his head, it only required some time and effort to understand it.

Bogo looked like his head was going to burst, "This is too much! I'd prefer not knowing," he wailed. He was familiar with the rudiments of Feesiks, which he had read about in Professor Helmsman's books, but this was all too much for him now. His nerves were very frayed, especially as result of having nearly lost his fear.

"So we need to find the Monk, who is a member of this ancient, but now defunct sect, who used to use Karaoke to combat Boredom. I don't understand why? What could we use him for, we have this Machine you talk of. You have years of extensive scientific research into Feesiks. Why do we need this old religious book?" asked Fiengus.

"I was sceptical too, Fiengus. But, there are too many parallels with the discoveries that we have made. We were dealing with pure science and for the first time what we were saying echoed what was being said by religion. This could not be ignored. This book, although badly named, is very important to our current crisis. There's a passage that prophesises what is happening and we need the Monk to help us interpret it," said Professor Helmsman.

"What's so important about this passage?" asked Bogo inquisitively.

"It contains a prophecy that talks of how a man will come to save us all from a great danger. It contains, we believe, the answer as to how to defeat the force behind the *Instances*. It really is our only hope; even the discipline of Feesiks can't answer this question. It is imperative that we find out what this passage means," replied Professor Kinootz, looking very serious and anxious.

"Ok, where will we find this Monk?" asked Fiengus.

"He resides in a mountain top retreat, secluded away from the outside world," answered Professor Helmsman. Both Fiengus and Bogo burst out laughing. "What?" asked Professor Helmsman.

Fiengus and Bogo looked at one another and said "Cliché!"

16 THE MONK

Fiengus, Bogo and Professor Helmsman set out for the Monk's mountain top retreat, leaving the other professors to work on the Machine. Both Fiengus and Bogo were annoyed at not getting to see the Machine and told Professor Helmsman about how much they hated his keeping things from them. He told them that they were impatient and it would all happen in good time. This formed much of their conversation as they made their way up the mountain path, which led to the top of the mountain. The view from halfway up, where they camped for the night, revealed the isolation in which they lived in Von Dufflestein, there was nothing but hills and vast forests on one side, then the sea which stretched out infinitely on the other. The nearest town was only visible from further up the mountain, the town of Von Dunkenstein. Fiengus had only visited there once and the recollection made him shudder. It was a strange and backward place.

They stopped for a rest some two thirds up, having set out early that morning, and gazed up at the still distant summit. Fiengus and Professor Helmsman remarked at the unspoiled beauty that surrounded them, the constant reminder that they were only a small and insignificant part of a far greater whole, but that nonetheless there was a comfort in at least experiencing this. Their philosophising was cut short by a panic attack that Bogo started having about altitude sickness and vertigo. They decided to press on and sedated Bogo with a stick to the back of the head. The going was slow and tough, as Bogo weighed considerably more than they anticipated. When they were about out of hope and had considered rolling Bogo back down and continuing without him they suddenly found themselves at the top.

They gazed at a large building, which resembled a picture of an Asian Temple that Fiengus had seen. "This is it," said Professor Helmsman, "this is the temple of the Monk."

"I hope he's in," said Fiengus who was feeling exhausted.

"I never thought about that. We really should have called. Quick let's find out." They ran to the door and knocked, then waited feeling impatient that it be opened soon. The door opened very suddenly with no one visible behind it. "Hello," called out Professor Helmsman. No answer came, "I guess we just go in." They entered the vast hallway, dragging Bogo behind them, and saw before them sitting on a glass block, almost giving the impression of levitation but not quite convincingly enough, the man they took to be the Monk.

"Welcome," said the Monk. "I've been expecting you. Please have a seat and...what happened to him?" he asked pointing suddenly at Bogo.

"Oh, eh he passed out from altitude sickness," answered Professor Helmsman quickly. He decided to change the subject, "Oh great and wise one, we come seeking guidance. This is Fiengus Longfinger..."

"I know," said the Monk, "and the silent one is Bogo Snot Troll. I also know why you are here, but you do not, for you seek guidance about a passage in *The Story of Life*, but it is not for me to tell you. You seek someone else or something else to be exact." He moved slowly towards them and placed a hand on each of their shoulders, with the obvious exception of Bogo's shoulders, and smiled, "Come and I will show you the way."

He led them through the temple, which was adorned with pictures, depicting great events from the birth of the universe. There was a strangeness to the place, it all seemed very other worldly yet familiar. This was disconcerting as Fiengus had never been or even heard about this place in his life. As they continued through, Fiengus stopped suddenly and stared at an etching carved into a pillar that showed a human like figure with a long spiralling finger. "What is this?" he asked completely taken aback.

"This?" answered the Monk "This is one of the gods of Longfinger. They are among the most ancient of the spectral beings. They were there at the beginning, were instrumental in it. They point the way for us all. You bear their mark on you," he then pointed at Fiengus' finger; as if it weren't clear enough to everyone there.

"I knew it was a gift from the gods that I had, but never knew this," said Fiengus, looking intently at the carving. He stared intently at the figure depicted in the carving and felt strangely like he knew him.

"The finger is just a mark, but it is not the gift. That is something else you must discover," said the Monk, who then turned round and continued before Fiengus could ask further questions. They came to a small, black door which opened out onto a balcony, overlooking the surrounding mountains and hills. As they stepped out a strong wind swept through them, causing Bogo to stir slightly and mutter something about butterflies. Luckily he was still slightly sedated and made little noise, despite seeming to be having night terrors. The Monk closed the door and then walked over to the balustrade and looked out over the land. "It is beautiful is it not? But it is not all there is, there is a whole world of infinite beauty out there for us to discover. We just need to have the right eyes to see it."

"Are you going to teach us how to see it?" asked Fiengus, who was feeling that this was a little abstract. He also felt that the Monk was saying a lot of this purely for effect and that it was becoming like a tour of some old castle.

"No. I am only going to show the way, I can do no more," replied the Monk, smiling in a way he would have hoped would come across as mysterious, but stirred in Fiengus an impression of smugness.

"What must we do?" asked Fiengus, "We desperately need answers, the world is in danger!"

"Fiengus, you are seeking to save the world, because you feel that you must, but this is not so. You do this because you choose to do it. You must believe that you can do it, and then simply do it."

"But, we don't know what must be done," pleaded Professor Helmsman. "This passage in the Story of Life, it talks of a man who will come and stop a great and destructive force from the stars. It talks of a power that seeks to destroy the earth, but is repelled by its opposing force, but that eventually the time will come when this force is too weak, it says 'when men and women turn from the force of Fun and are driven by other desires and wants, they will forget and will be forgotten.' This is happening and I think the man might be Fiengus. It says 'he will come and will bear resemblance to the gods, but will have a true gift none shall see, but all shall witness.' I think he," pointing at Fiengus, "will save us, and that the book is telling us this."

The Monk looked at him, then Fiengus and smiled. "I can only show you the way; you will have to create your own answers to these questions."

"You mean find, don't you," questioned Fiengus, who was becoming annoyed now and wanted a straight answer.

The Monk did not answer, but merely turned and climbed on top of the balustrade of the balcony and said, "All that is required is a leap of faith." He then leapt from the balcony. Fiengus and Professor Helmsman rushed to the edge, but were too late. The Monk was gone.

"What in the name! He just leaped off. I thought this guy was a bit weird but this?" said Fiengus, who was walking back and forth, checking over the edge occasionally.

"Fiengus, I know what we must do," said Professor Helmsman, looking suddenly very animated and bright eyed. "The Monk wants us to jump!"

"No way! You must be kidding, you're a man of science and you're going to do this?" cried out Fiengus. He had grabbed Professor Helmsman by the shoulders, to emphasise his point and also to hold him back from the edge.

"Come on, the Monk may seem crazy, but I've read the book, there are too many coincidences. We have to do this Fiengus," replied Professor Helmsman, looking directly at Fiengus and looking elated.

"Look, this is insane; no wonder there are only one of these guys, if they all jump off of mountains to prove a point. Now there are none and you want us to join them in a nice heap at the bottom. No thank you."

"Fiengus, you must believe, from what I have read, from what I have seen there can be no doubt."

"It is absolutely absurd, how can jumping of a mountain give us the answers to saving the world. This is just like those cults, which all get together, talking about going into space to meet the grand creator or something and all end up drinking cups of tea laced with arsenic. It's crazy!" cried out Fiengus.

"Of course it seems absurd, but don't you see, everything up till now has been absurd." Fiengus looked over the edge and shuddered. He was being won over by the idea. The Professor was right, everything had been absurd, almost to the point of being unbelievable.

"Ok let's do it. But just one thing though, just to be sure," said Fiengus.

"What is that?" asked Professor Helmsman. Fiengus then whispered into his ear and they then looked at one another in agreement. "You're right Fiengus, let's do it."

Bogo began to gain consciousness, having the sensation of being moved. He suddenly realised he was sitting upright on what looked like a balcony. Fiengus and Professor Helmsman were supporting him by his shoulders. "Hey, guys, what's going on? Why I am sitting on a balustrade on top of a mountain?" They looked at him, then one another and nodded, "Guys..." Bogo felt them push and he suddenly had a falling sensation and he watched the balcony very quickly get further away, the faces of his two friends who had just pushed him looked down at him, expectantly. Then something very strange happened to him.

Some time passed and Professor Helmsman and Fiengus waited anxiously. "Oh, what if we are wrong about this?" asked Fiengus. "We just shoved Bogo of a mountain, because of something you read in a book and a crazy hermit told us to do." The faith he had had was quickly disappearing and doubt was setting in.

"Have faith Fiengus," said Professor Helmsman, but not as convincingly as Fiengus had hoped. He then peered over the edge and then said "Look, I think I can see him, he's ok, I think he's trying to signal to us. He's waving." Fiengus looked over and could vaguely make out Bogo, alive and gesturing towards them.

"Eh, I don't think he's waving, I think he might be a little angry to be honest," said Fiengus, who had more accurately interpreted Bogo's signalling.

"Probably, but he'll understand. He missed most of what the Monk said so this probably makes no sense to him."

"I heard everything the Monk said and this still makes no sense. Poor Bogo, we'll need to make this up to him, somehow." Fiengus then looked at Professor Helmsman and said, "So who goes next?" There was a long and uncomfortable silence, eventually broken by Professor Helmsman.

"Ok, I will go next, but you have to follow." He then climbed on top of the balustrade and looked out, then turned his head to Fiengus, "Might be easier if you push." At this Fiengus pushed the Professor. He then suddenly felt very alone. The edge of the balcony seemed to beckon, like a wasp nest does to a small, inquisitive child.

"What am I doing here?" he asked himself, then ran towards the edge and jumped.

17 THE REALITY OF A PI

Alfitch sat in his office, thinking. He stared at the phone. It was clear that he needed Hyacinth's help, but to admit that he had failed, was wrong, was very difficult for him. Before becoming a private detective he had never failed at anything. Now this, his first case, had all gone terribly wrong. He took his eyes off the phone and looked hard into the mirror. The trench coat, the trilby, brogues, the accent, the whole thing was not him. He threw the hat onto his desk. It was what he had always sought out, failure, but he didn't like the cost, the lives, and the people that were affected by it. It was too difficult.

Picking up the phone he dialled Hyacinth. She answered, saying his name, as though she knew it would be him. "Yes it's me. As you know, I got the wrong guy," he started struggling with the words. "I messed up. I'm going to return your money... I just don't know how to solve this one."

The voice of Hyacinth came through, "Listen to me, get yourself together and meet me down stairs in half an hour."

"But I said I quit, I'm... not cut out for this."

"Quit with the feeling sorry, so you got it wrong, do you just quit? I need you, we are going to confront the Mayor and I need you there in case it gets heavy. Can I rely on you?"

Alfitch looked at himself in the mirror again, staring into his own eyes. Could he do this, could he do this one thing? He turned around grabbed his trilby and said, "See you in half an hour." He then put down the phone, opened a drawer and stuck a picture of Humphrey Bogart up, covering the mirror. Something stirred in him. He was going to do this one time, this detective thing and he was going to do it right. He pulled down the blinds, cutting the light into slices, turned on a jazz record and lit a cigarette using his desk lighter. "All I owe them is one good performance," he said to himself. Drawing on the cigarette he suddenly started coughing and spluttering. He quickly stubbed it out in an ashtray. "A step too far, maybe, disgusting." He said aloud to himself.

18 REVELATIONS

The air rushed against Fiengus' face as he plummeted down, towards what he now assumed was his foolish death when suddenly everything went strange...

Wow, I see the stars, I'm in the universe. No that sounds stupid, I'm always in the universe. Space, that's where I am, or at least like space, but this is different. I can see me! Oh, wait, it's not me it's the wood carving guy, the one the Monk spoke about. 'Fiengus Longfinger, you come here for a reason. What is it?' I'm here to find out what I must do to save the world. 'No you are not, you are here for something else.' I am? Yes I am. I want to know who I am, you see I'm in an existential quandary... thingy. I don't know what I'm supposed to do with my life or what to be. What do I do? 'Fiengus that is not for anyone to decide but you, you must make these choices for yourself and create yourself through them.' But it's hard to decide, there are so many choices. 'There are and you must make them unaided or else they are not your choices and you are not you.' This sort of helps, but I've been trying to work it out my entire life, won't you just tell me? 'No. Fiengus you're time here is over you must return and find these things out for yourself...'

Fiengus found himself lying on the ground at the foot the mountain. He could feel the earth and smell the grass underneath and he could see the 8ft Bogo bounding towards him armed with a very large rock. "Run, Fiengus run!" a voice cried. Fiengus looked to the source of the exclamation and saw Professor Helmsman up a tree, "He's mad, Fiengus really mad!"

"I'm going to kill you Fiengus Longfinger!" cried out Bogo who then launched the rock at him. It narrowly missed and Fiengus was up in a flash, running for his life. It was some time before they both talked Bogo around.

As it transpired, it was not so much the pushing him off the balcony that had infuriated Bogo so much, but more that he no longer felt fear. The shock of falling and the ensuing meeting he had with the Spectral Beings had somehow relieved him of his interminable fear. Bogo was of course furious about this; he had worked for years perfecting his cowardice and now it was gone, ruined and he would now return home, if that were even an option now, a shame to his family once more. "Bogo," said Professor Helmsman, "you can't live your life in fear anyway, you should be happy that you are free from it."

"That's what the Spectral Beings said," replied Bogo, who now sat staring into the distance. "When I had the fear I had something, I knew where I was, but that's gone and now I have to start out all over again."

"What will you do?" asked Fiengus. "You surely don't want to become a coward again, do you?" Bogo turned to look at Fiengus, and then turned his head away once more.

"I don't know. You know the strangest thing about all of this? It's that I now have the strongest fear in my life, the fear of the unknown, the uncertainty of what to do with my life." As Bogo said this Fiengus rose and walked over to him and sat beside him.

"Bogo, I know this fear, I've avoided it all my life too, but you can't let someone else make these decisions for you, like you let your family do to you. They should respect you for what you become, the choices you make."

"Is that how it is for you Fiengus," said Bogo looking him in the eye, seeking reassurance. Fiengus was taken aback by the question.

"No Bogo, but I don't let it stop me. It's for me to make these decisions and not anyone else, or else I lose myself." They then looked out into the distance and thought about the events and choices they had made up until this point. Professor Helmsman then came over and looked at them.

"Doesn't anyone want to know what the Spectral Beings said to me?" he asked sounding a little desperate and left out.

Professor Helmsman told them that in his vision the Spectral Beings had told him that 'men rarely do as is set in the stars,' that 'they choose their own path.' He had asked them, does this not make the prophesy in the book redundant. They had replied: 'You could look at it this way, but the prophesy was not meant to be taken literally, more as a possible path. There were others of course, lots, but to fit them in to one book was unrealistic.' After some more discussion about this, the conclusion was that yes, the prophesy was a bit of a waste of time and that basically they were on their own. This was the end of his vision and he now felt that really this had been a total waste of time. At this Bogo leapt to his feet.

"Rubbish! I've not gone through all this, having been nearly killed numerous times, pushed off of balconies, dealt with the mentally unhinged for you to tell me that it was all for nothing!" shouted Bogo, with so much force that both Professor Helmsman and Fiengus were taken aback.

"But how do we stop these *Instances* when we haven't a clue what they really are. We were banking on a prophecy that as it turns out is of no truth whatsoever!" pleaded Professor Helmsman. Bogo grabbed him by the collar and looked him dead in the eye.

"Then we make it true!"

"Wow, I like the new Bogo," said Fiengus, sounding impressed. "Yeah let's do it, let's make the prophecy true and beat whatever or whoever is behind these *Instances* into...well wherever. Bogo what would you say?"

"I'd say let's crush them," he roared and threw Professor Helmsman into the air, leaving him sprawled on the ground then turned and strode purposefully off.

"Where to Bogo?" asked Fiengus.

"The one place we'll get straight answers. The University," replied Bogo.

"I'm not sure," said Professor Helmsman, picking himself up from the ground and brushing himself down, "they're even more obscure in the Feesiks department than the Monk." They looked at each other in silent agreement then hurried off after Bogo. Whether or not this was the correct path they were on, they were certainly on it now, following an 8ft troll, who was having an identity crisis. What could go wrong?

19 THE MAYOR'S CONFESSION

Alfitch had picked up Hyacinth and was now driving into the centre of town. He looked at her then asked, "So where we going and why?" She took out a small mirror and began applying powder to her cheeks, giving the impression of blushing. She did this slowly and deliberately, much to the annoyance of Alfitch. "Look lady, talk or I'm pulling over and you're getting out." Hyacinth snapped the mirror shut and then looked to him.

"Well, I've been thinking over everything that happened, again and again and some things just didn't add up." She adjusted herself in her seat and watched Alfitch's attention peak before continuing. "Firstly, I overheard my husband remark, on the night of his disappearance, that he hadn't seen the person at the door for some time. I had heard him saying this, but only recalled it recently. This made me think about the sort of people my husband knows. You see, he works all the time, his department sorts out issues, mostly internal, within the Mayor's office. The Mayor makes a lot of errors of judgement and it's their department's job to sort them out. He is always working and doesn't really socialise much. So I figured that this person could be someone he has worked with before. The second thing was the conversation I had with the Mayor. I had mentioned that someone new had taken over at the Sorting Office and when he heard the name Von Staninces he immediately leapt to his feet and looked incredibly worried. He had called the guy he hired, Fiengus Longfinger, and warned him of the danger he was in."

"Ok, he calls up this Fiengus to warn him, so?"

"Well, don't you see, how could he have known that Fiengus would be in danger just from hearing a name, a name that he shouldn't even recognise."

"So you think the Mayor knows this guy Von Staninces?" asked Alfitch, looking intently at her, with a brow furrowed by thought.

"I do. And there is one more thing I have worked out, the name

Von Staninces, it's an anagram."

"A what?"

"You know a word made from mixing up the letters of another word."

"Oh, yeah," said Alfitch. "So it's an anagram of what?"

"Staninces is an anagram of Instances." Alfitch thought all this over for some time while Hyacinth proceeded to tell him about her going to see the Mayor and the arrival of Von Staninces.

Alfitch looked at her and said, "So the Mayor is being forced into something, something dark, probably in too deep now to get out. He gets shot by this Von Staninces and doesn't say a thing. You got to have a lot on a guy to pull a stunt like that."

"You are right and that is why we are going to the Mayor's office. We've got some questions for him," she said.

"And I know just how to ask them," said Alfitch with a steely look in his eyes. All this corruption and deceit was getting to him. Something powerful was building in him. He gripped the steering wheel hard as he drove towards the Mayor's office, towards what he hoped would be the truth about all this.

The Mayor sat in his office, which was in even more disarray than usual. He was sweating and looked incredibly shabby; his clothes looked like he had been sleeping in them, but he looked as though he hadn't slept in a long time. His left arm was in a sling, the result of the gunshot wound he had received. He was staring at the wall when the phone rang and caused him to leap forward. He answered it and gingerly said, "Mayor's office." On the other end he heard a voice he recognised immediately, causing a spasm of fear to shoot through him. "What do you want?" he asked, sounding defeated and nothing like his usual boisterous overconfident self. The voice on the other end began to talk and his face dropped as he slipped back into his chair. "Look, I can't, I can't," he pleaded and he almost began to shake with terror. The voice made more demands, but the Mayor continued to intone, "No, I won't do it. Too many people have been hurt already. I'm not doing it," he then slammed down the phone, taking himself by surprise. "Oh god, what have I done," he picked up the phone and was about to call back when the door to his office was thrown open and a man he did not recognise came rushing in towards him, followed by the voice of his assistant, "You haven't got an appointment!" He thought that this was it; they were here to take him too, when he saw Hyacinth enter, which took him by surprise, but before he could say anything Alfitch had him by the collar and was dragging him to the window.

He found himself hanging upside down outside of his window, somewhere unfamiliar to him. "What do you want?" he cried out pleadingly.

"I ask the questions, right?" said Alfitch.

"Ok, ok!" pleaded the Mayor.

"Tell me what you really know about the *Instances* and how do you know this Von Staninces?" said Alfitch gruffly. The Mayor proceeded to confess all he knew. It transpired that he had been approached by Von Staninces who told the Mayor that if he did not comply with everything he said he would reveal sensitive information about the Mayor, which would show him to be completely inept and incompetent at his job. This would bring shame upon him and cost him his job. The Mayor said he was terrified as his family had grown accustomed to the lifestyle he could give them in his position, but without the job he was nothing. He'd agreed, thinking that they were probably like all the others who had bribed and extorted him in the past and just wanted a prominent position for their son or daughter or a blind eye passed on the building of a nuclear power plant in a school playground. But it was more. The next day several men and women came around unexpectedly and introduced themselves as new heads of departments and when the Mayor had checked on the current occupants of these positions, they were all gone, had vanished overnight. He knew that things had gone pretty far, but then the *Instances* started and other people started vanishing. He'd been forced into closing the research on Karaoke and then members of the team working on this began to disappear. He was then told to hire someone to investigate the *Instances*, as if they were seen to be doing nothing suspicion would be aroused. So according to their criteria he was to find someone incompetent, useless and who would ultimately uncover nothing of the truth. He hired Fiengus Longfinger, who was the son of a rich family and a layabout. He'd then sent some information, most of which was of little importance to some troll and then sent Fiengus off on a wild goose chase to retrieve it. However, Von Staninces had informed him that he had heard that Fiengus was making headway, had already drawn the conclusion that he should take the information to the Feesiks department and a friend he had there. This he said was unacceptable and he would have to take matters into his own hands. He said he felt terrible, Fiengus seemed a nice enough guy and this Von Staninces was going to kill him and when he heard from Hyacinth that Fiengus was going to the sorting office, the very office where Von Staninces was working he'd panicked. He did not want any bloodshed. When Fiengus returned he'd told him to go to the University, he knew that if Von Staninces found out he would kill him, but he knew that he had to try something to stop them, before it was too late.

"There's something more you can do," said Alfitch, who had pulled the Mayor back into his office and was sitting in a chair opposite him. The Mayor looked worriedly at him, "You can finish these guys off. Call in the *Department of Correction* to arrest these men and redeem yourself. We can then question those who are here about any others and where they have all those people they have snatched." The Mayor looked at him and thought it through, then looked at Alfitch.

"Let's do it. This is what I do best, clear up big messes like this." He leaped from his chair, but immediately sunk back into it. "But what about Von Staninces, he's one nasty piece of work."

Alfitch looked at him then moved closer and said, "He hasn't met me though." The Mayor looked at the short man sitting in front of him and almost wavered, but something told him to trust this man, despite his stature.

"Ok, you'll find him here. He just called and wanted me to meet him. I'd refused, but can call him back, make some excuse and then arrange it. You come with me and take him by surprise and grab him. Meanwhile, I'll get the *Department of Correction* down here pronto." He then picked up the phone and dialled Von Staninces number and as the phone rang he felt something strange; this was the first time he had ever made a good decision in his life and he liked it, even though it may lead to his death.

The ringing stopped and a voice on the other end said, "So you've changed your mind then? And here was me thinking you needed another reminder of who you take orders from."

"Yes," said the Mayor looking at Alfitch, "I have. Tell me where to meet you."

They had arranged to meet Von Staninces at the harbour that evening and were now there. Alfitch had taken up position on top of a large boathouse, giving him a clear view of the Mayor. As they waited Alfitch looked out over the sea and gazed at a specific point, a place where his home had once been. His reminiscing was cut short when he saw car headlights coming in their direction. He slipped out of sight and observed from above.

The car pulled to a stop and Von Staninces got out, leaving the lights on, making it easier for Alfitch to watch. From his position above he couldn't make out the conversation, but he could tell that Von Staninces was not happy about something. He began pointing and shouting at the Mayor then drew a pistol from his jacket and pointed it at the Mayor, who began to plead with him. He then began to march him towards the peer. Alfitch knew that there was little time to act and knew exactly what he had to do. He did something he hadn't done in public for a very long time and threw off his long jacket revealing a pair of very large white wings and then he threw himself off the building opening the wings revealing their expansive span. Swooping down on the unsuspecting Von Staninces he knocked him from his feet, the gun flying harmlessly from his hand, knocking him unconscious. The Mayor looked incredibly stunned then very relieved.

"Alfitch, you saved me!" he cried, and then staring at his

wings said, "Your wings, I know who you are. But, it can't be, I read about you as a child. You're Alfitch, but I mean the really famous one." Alfitch looked at him, looking far larger and revealing not only his fantastic wings but an incredibly muscular physique. He looked like a miniature Adonis with wings.

"I am Alfitch, and I have kept that a secret for a very long time and now I am forced to reveal it once more to the world." His voice too had changed, the terrible faux American accent was gone and he spoke with a clear and pure voice.

"You were a warrior, from an ancient civilisation that was destroyed by a volcano. Only you survived and then disappeared. And here you are! It was thought you were just a myth. Why are you pretending to be a detective?" asked an enamoured, but perplexed Mayor.

"I was the greatest warrior there ever was, I was born this way, a gift from the gods. It was easy. I vanquished armies; many came to test themselves against me, but all perished. But it was too easy. To be the best at something is lonely and begins to get tedious and lack challenge. I also got reckless: I had so many followers and we set up a city, named it after me and it was perfect, the greatest city in the world. But, foolishly and arrogantly I had built it on top of an active volcano and then, well as you know everything disappeared the day it erupted. I felt terrible about it and to relieve my guilt I disappeared and created new guises for myself, testing myself by trying things I wasn't good at, avoiding using my gifts that had made things so easy. And here I am today, and I reveal my true self to you." The Mayor looked confused.

"But why call yourself Alfitch, if you wanted to avoid attention?"

"I went by many other names, but recently I have begun using my real name. It seemed to mean less to people these days, less significant, except to myself."

"Wow, that's quite a story. What now?" asked the Mayor.

Alfitch looked out to sea, the same feeling returning to him, and then he looked at the Mayor. "I feel I have had some part to play in sorting out these *Instances*. As best I could as a private detective. Perhaps I will become Alfitch again." He looked to the Mayor, walked over and placed a hand on his shoulder. "But for now, it is up to you to sort out this mess you have made." He then turned, stretched out his wings and flew off in the direction he had been looking, out to sea.

The Mayor watched him for some time, until he was invisible to him then turned and looked at Von Staninces. He knew that he had made a terrible mess, and this wasn't just a one off, his entire life had been one of getting by on luck and chance and more than a little corruption. He saw that this was a chance to redeem himself, but one that required effort. He picked out his phone and called someone from the *Department of Correction* who informed him that the names he'd given had been arrested and that they would send some agents out to him immediately. The Mayor looked out to sea and felt for the first time a sense of pride, something unique to him and one he relished.

20 THE MACHINE

Fiengus, Bogo and Professor Helmsman were back at the University and were discussing with the other professors exactly what they had discovered. They sat around the grand table and it was the first time that Fiengus noticed that several chairs lay vacant, their regular occupants not present. "Well, really the whole trip up the mountain was a waste of time," said Professor Helmsman.

"Yeah, we basically learned that we had to figure this out by ourselves and that the prophecy was meaningless," added Fiengus.

Bogo looked around the room at the professors, then sat forward, leaning on the table, causing it too creak under his muscular weight and announced, "We never needed the prophecy, what we need is some guts to do this. We have the Machine, we have Fiengus one of the greatest singers of Karaoke I've ever heard and we've got you lot, the greatest minds in the entire world." As though perfectly timed, they heard a scream, followed by a loud crashing sound. Everyone looked towards an open window, where Professor Nigel had been previously. They rushed to the window and saw him in a heap of hair and man, his fall having been broken by a car. A few moments later, Professor Nigel appeared to regain consciousness and began hitting the car, crying out that whoever had parked it there would suffer. They returned to sitting around the table and resumed their conversation. The professors looked around and began to chat amongst themselves animatedly.

"We just can't expect all the answers to be in one book. We can do this, whatever it is that needs to be done," said Fiengus, who now felt inspired by Bogo.

"And what do we need to do?" asked one of the professors.

"Figure it out. We can't keep expecting someone else to come up with the answers. It's up to us," replied Bogo. Fiengus looked around at the worried expression on the faces of the professors. Bogo's new found courage was inspiring, but his relentless single mindedness was something that worried the professors. They were concerned and rightly so that if they got this wrong then everyone could pay as result.

Fiengus decided on another tactic, "What have you discovered, since we have been away? I mean is the Machine operational?"

One of the professors answered, "Yes, we've run some tests and it seems to be working at a far higher level of performance than before. I've attached the dance mat and I can work it, but the ABBA..." the professor stopped talking and she looked around as though seeking support from her colleagues. "Well, it certainly helps, but none of us can sing it, the range is too great." At this the professors began crying out about the failure of the ABBA project.

"Yes it's too difficult!" piped up one.

"It's impossible," said another.

"Well, did you do it as a duet?" intervened Fiengus, causing a murmur amongst the professors.

"What do you mean?" asked one of them.

"I mean that there were two singers in ABBA, you can't hope to harness its power with only one vocalist. Bogo and me did it pretty well, he's a great falsetto." This caused Bogo to beam with pride and look to his friend.

"It's true, Fiengus and I were pretty damn good, we got people joining in and even caused a man to leap out of a window," said Bogo.

"And not just to prove a scientific theory either," added Fiengus.

"Well then you two should try it out," said a professor. The other professors began to agree and looked like their spirits were lifted.

"Yes, yes, you must try!" cried out one, leaping from his chair.

"To the laboratory!" They cried out together. The whole group then left and walked down the corridor in the direction of the laboratory.

Inside the laboratory they were greeted by a smell that took Fiengus back to his days at school, the aroma of sulphur, phosphorous, burning magnesium, copper sulphate and singed school ties. He was in awe, he had always really loved science, the experimentation, the ideas, the explosions, the answers that could be revealed from simple ideas, how the whole universe could be explained by some numbers and symbols in a way that he never really understood, but appreciated completely. The room had vast jars, vials, beakers of innumerable size and shape, with strange coloured liquids bubbling away and emitting odorous gasses.

His reminiscing was brought to a halt by the unveiling of the Machine. The professors were all gathered around and were looking incredibly pleased with themselves. A sense of pride was palpable in the room and Fiengus was very excited. Professor Helmsman stood next to him and whispered, "This is it Fiengus, the end result of years of research and millions of investment. You are honoured to see this." Fiengus' eyes lit up and then the machine was unveiled.

Before him was something that resembled a small cassette player, something he had only read about in books, with a very small screen on it. It was made of plastic and the tape deck was held together by masking tape. In the centre was a single speaker and attached was a small microphone. The Machine had been hooked up to a dance mat that looked like it belonged to an old console system. Fiengus struggled to hide his disappointment, while the professors looked to him expectantly. "What do you think?" asked one of them.

"It's eh, compact isn't it? Is that tape?" said Fiengus, who was struggling to find positives.

"Oh, yes that is. We had an accident and dropped the Machine. Works alright though," replied the professor.

"There's a dance mat. That's nice," commented Fiengus, trying really hard now not to cry.

A professor stepped forward and said, "That was my

addition, I operate the dance mat," she said with beaming pride.

"Oh. Excellent. There is only one microphone?"

"Yes, but we've sent Professor Hawks to find another. I can't wait to see what you can do with this. It's so exciting." At this they began the preparations. The second microphone was attached, some new AA batteries added to the Machine, a tape inserted into the front and finally it was switched on. The small screen lit up and a small circle of light began to grow until the whole screen was lit. After this a small oriental looking man appeared and then said, "Welcome to Karaoke," then bowed and disappeared as the image panned to the left and was replaced by a scene from a beach.

"It is ready!" said Professor Helmsman dramatically. Bogo and Fiengus stepped forward and looked to one another. The professor who operated the dance mat stepped forward and took up position. The mat had arrows pointing in various directions, and in different colours.

"I'm Professor Beeswax by the way," she said as she began to stretch off. She had tied a sweat band around her head and looked ready for action.

One of the professors placed a jar in front of the Machine, and then quickly stepped away. "This is a sample of concentrated Boredom we have collected. We can measure the effect caused by the Machine afterwards."

"Ok, are you guys ready?" asked Professor Helmsman.

Bogo and Fiengus looked at one another and then stepped forward, grabbed a microphone each and said, "Let's do this."

The Machine kicked into action and the intro chords to ABBA's *Gimme! Gimme! Gimme! (A Man After Midnight)* began. The lights of Professor Beeswax's mat began changing, keeping to the rhythm of the song. As the galloping bass line kicked in leading to the descending initial vocal lines, the room began to suddenly emanate a very powerful and visible force. Professors were dancing uncontrollably and people were entering the room and joining in.

The janitor flew across the room, riding on his wheeled bucket using his mop as a dance partner. The room had erupted into a party of spontaneous and incredible power. Professor Beeswax was dancing like a celestial movement, of elegance and pure unadulterated rhythm and poise. And there, right in the centre of it, in the calm eye of this tornado of jubilation were Bogo and Fiengus, singing with all the gusto of a drunk at midnight walking back from the pub.

Then three and a half minutes later it was over. The dancing stopped, but the room still smouldered over with the remnants of what had just unfolded in that room. The sample jar was gone, had vanished completely only a small mark on the floor told of its ever being there.

"Well, did it work?" asked Fiengus.

The results of the experiment were phenomenal. The sample of concentrated Boredom was not merely altered as had been hoped, but completely destroyed. The force produced was so powerful that its effects were felt within an 8 mile radius. People had taken to the streets and began partying, the students living around the University, partied even harder than normal. The aftershock was still being felt, people were smiling everywhere and were just genuinely happy. It was something to behold. Professor Helmsman and several others were deep in discussion, leaving Bogo and Fiengus some chill out time. This however, was cut short by the ringing of Fiengus' phone.

"Hey you've changed your ringtone, Fiengus," said an observant Bogo.

"Yes, I thought I'd better. That's quite a power we unleashed there. We'd better be careful." Bogo nodded in agreement. Fiengus then answered the phone, "It's the Mayor," he said to Bogo, who looked over intently.

On the other end the Mayor's voice could be heard, "Look Fiengus I'm going to come clean. I hired you under orders from Von Staninces. They had taken control here and I was too afraid to do anything about it. I'm sorry; I never thought that your life would be in danger because of it."

"Why did they want me?" asked a confused Fiengus.

"Well, they wanted someone incompetent, totally and utterly useless, a total loser they said..." answered the Mayor.

"Ok, ok," interrupted a hurt Fiengus, "why me though?" However, even as he asked this he knew the answer.

"But, Fiengus they were wrong. I was. You've done great work. It's just you know, you were a bit of a layabout."

"Hey! That's because I just didn't know what I wanted to do with myself." He knew though that it was true. He had been afraid to do anything. It all seemed to be such a big thing, to decide your whole life, to decide what to be. It occurred to him now that there really wasn't this big decision, but life was in fact a series of decisions, ones that you could get wrong and inevitably would do, but there were no final decisions and no ultimate answers either.

"Look Fiengus, we were wrong about you. But anyway, back to the main point," Fiengus couldn't help but notice that the Mayor sounded more assertive, more in control than he had ever been. "We've caught Von Staninces and the members of his group that were working for him here. They are in custody and are being prepped for questioning. I thought that you'd like to come along and hear what they have to say. It should shed some light on these *Instances*."

Fiengus agreed that he would head over and was leaving the Feesiks department when one of the younger professors, Professor Fuirk, came running over to him. "Fiengus, we've been examining the strange pattern in the map, the one we thought had some significance," he said, looking a little out of breath having run from the other end of the room, which wasn't particularly far away.

"Yes," replied Fiengus, "and what did you find?" He looked expectantly at Professor Fuirk.

"We found nothing. The pattern was just random, we tried constellations, we tried triangulating the points, but nothing came up. They were just random."

"I could have sworn that there was a pattern there."

"So could we, but I guess it's just one of those things." This didn't help. It was one of those phrases that said very little, if anything at all. Professor Fuirk could see that this hadn't satisfied Fiengus so he added, "Fiengus, people often see patterns in very random things; they really want them to mean something, but most of the time they don't. It's just something we do, try to attach meaning to something that has none. But hey, on the positive side it didn't reveal anything that should worry us, the opposite really."

Fiengus thanked Professor Fuirk, then left, taking Professor Helmsman's car. Fiengus thought about what the professor had said, about things being random and our attaching meaning to them. Was his life like this, he thought, a series of random acts, with no significance at all. His feeling of existential angst was returning again, but he quelled it by thinking about the purpose he felt he had. He was part of something bigger than himself and this certainly made him feel better. He focussed on this and wondered what this Von Staninces had to say.

21 ANOTHER INTERROGATION

Fiengus was sitting outside the cell which Von Staninces was being detained in. He was being questioned by some police officers while Fiengus, the Mayor and several other men who worked for the *Department of Correction*, were observing him through one way glass. Von Staninces was one tough guy, he wouldn't talk, but merely smiled at each successive officer who came in and questioned him.

"Oh, this is no use," remarked the Mayor, looking very irritated, "Can't we just beat him up or something, you know like they do in movies. With phone books or something?"

"Of course not, Mayor, that just isn't allowed," replied one of the officers.

"But we need him to talk. Peoples' lives are in danger." The Mayor was looking on the point of defeat; they had been at it for several hours now. Fiengus looked at Von Staninces intently through the glass. He was thinking about something deeply, and barely noticed the argument that had broken out between the Mayor and the officers.

Calmly he said over the top of the group, "Can we play some music to the detainee?" The argument stopped and everyone in the room looked to Fiengus.

One officer, named Hansvere, looked at him, removed his hat and remarked sarcastically, "Yeah and you can give him a foot massage too while you're at it." The other officers laughed, but the Mayor looked thoughtful for a moment.

"Wait," said the Mayor, "I think we should give him a chance. Let him have a try. You lot have been at this for hours and have gotten nowhere."

Officer Hansvere looked a little offended at this and then placed his hat back on and walked over to Fiengus, "Ok then, tell me what you want. You got five minutes with him."

Fiengus smiled, "I only need 2 minutes and 47 seconds," the officer looked confused, "and an MP3 player."

Fiengus entered the room with Von Staninces, who was sitting behind a table, and was being held down by chains. He looked initially confused by Fiengus' entrance, but quickly changed his expression to one of disdain. Fiengus sat opposite him and placed the MP3 player on the desk, then calmly walked around the table and plugged it in. He then very slowly took out his phone and searched through his music collection, taking his time and not once looking at Von Staninces. Von Staninces, looked confused, then sardonically asked, "What are you doing? What is this?" he was looking at the mirrored side of the one way glass.

"What's this lunatic doing?" asked officer Hansvere on the other side.

"Just wait," said the Mayor looking intently at Fiengus, who was now sitting down opposite Von Staninces and finally looked at him.

"Von Staninces, you are going to tell me everything you know about the *Instances,* where you've taken all these people and what this strange force coming towards Von Dufflestein is," said Fiengus very calmly.

Von Staninces looked at him then laughed, "Whatever are you talking about Fiengus Longfinger? Are you going to..."

"Have you ever heard of Napoleon?" Fiengus interrupted. "He led the French in the nineteenth century to almost complete control of Europe. He was a great man, but arrogant, thought he was invincible."

"What is this, a history lesson?" said Von Staninces moving slightly in his chair.

"Not really, what I'm trying to get at is this. He was such a great man, had a huge influence on the shaping of an entire continent, but it was not until the 4th of March 1974 that his influence was truly shown and his essence really captured."

"What are you talking about," said Von Staninces looking very confused.

Fiengus then pressed play on his MP3 player and just before the music started said, "Von Staninces what I am talking about is ABBA and *Waterloo*."

The track suddenly burst into life and Von Staninces let out a terrible scream, "No stop it stop, please..."

Officer Hansvere looked to the Mayor, looking completely shocked by what he was seeing. The other officers had begun tapping their feet, and then proceeded to join in at the chorus. Officer Hansvere then muttered, the words barely coming out, "Who, who is this guy?"

"Him? He's Fiengus Longfinger," replied the Mayor. They gazed in and watched as Fiengus paraded about the room singing along. Von Staninces had passed out and was lying face down on the table.

When he recovered he confessed everything he knew, the officer charged with taking the notes was completely shocked, as was everyone else there, by what they heard. What was written down was:

The detainee, one Von Staninces, made the following confession: I was sent here by my leaders to take over the central government of Von Dufflestein. We were to take up prominent positions and then cover up any information collected about our activities. It was known that some professors from a local university here had spotted our coming and we were to dispose of them and cover up the truth. To keep things seemingly normal we insisted that the Mayor hire someone to investigate the disappearances that we were behind, but stipulated that it had to be someone completely incompetent, who would find nothing out. We could not allow suspicion to be drawn, by having the Mayor's office seem to do nothing. However, this Fiengus that they hired was more effective than we thought. He drew conclusions we thought impossible and became a threat to our operation. I ordered that he be killed, but he eluded us. I had to go into hiding as I knew that my cover was blown. I organised to meet with the Mayor, who had outrun his uses and was going to dispose of him when I was knocked unconscious and brought here.

The detainee was then asked who his leaders were:

I work for a powerful force, the Legion of Borealis! They came to me and offered me great power, visited me in a dream. They are coming and there is nothing you can do NOTHING!!!!!

Von Staninces had then went into a frenzy and had to be sedated. He then revealed, under threat of more ABBA, where the Legion of Borealis were intending to attack. He said, "The Legion will come to the north, beyond the seas of this land. They will then come south like a wave and overwhelm us all, changing everything forever." He then put his head down, then looked up with tears in his eyes, "It's too late, there's nothing anyone can do." He was then taken away, after giving the location of the missing people.

"That's one messed up guy," said Officer Hansvere.

"He is now, but I knew him before," replied the Mayor, causing the officer to look at him in disbelief.

"You knew him before?"

"Yes, he used to work at the *Department of Correction*. When I was younger I used to go to clubs and things a lot and I used to meet up with him there, he was a karaoke singer. One of the best, before he just disappeared. This Legion must have got him and changed him somehow." The Mayor then turned away looking sad at the recollection then walked towards Fiengus. "Fiengus, do you think that you can stop this, the Legion of Borealis?"

Fiengus looked at him then replied, "I've seen the awesome power of Karaoke, I've also seen what people can do when they put their minds to it. Nothing is impossible if you believe, Mayor." He then turned and strode off, leaving the Mayor with a lot to think about.

Later that day the Mayor and his officers from the *Department of Correction* found and released all of the prisoners. They had been held in an old farm, just outside of Von Dufflestein. All the prisoners were very relieved and were in generally good health. Hyacinth had accompanied them also. She was very grateful and happy to see her husband again. As they embraced, he looked at her and said, "Hyacinth, I've had so much time to think about things, about us. I was thinking how I work all the time; have to have everything in such meticulous order and a perfect house, a perfect life as we seem to think. But, I have realised that it is not. We are forgetting to enjoy our lives and have fun!"

Hyacinth smiled at him and replied, "You are right, let's go on holiday, I think we've earned it." They both left, saying their goodbyes.

The Mayor found Von Snare, who greeted him warmly. "I'm glad you came around Mayor, and you sorted this out yourself too!" The Mayor ignored the condescension in the last remark and smiled at Von Snare.

"You were right Von Snare. You were always right, now that I think about it. In a strange way you would be a better mayor than me," he said sincerely and slightly sadly.

"Maybe before, but you seem changed Mayor, you seem to have found yourself, figured out what you're meant to be doing."

The Mayor reflected on this, then smiled and put his arm around Von Snare. "You are right again!" he laughed. They returned to the Mayor's office and began sorting out the mess that had been created and looked not to return things to how they were before, but to create them anew, with a new ideal.

22 FINAL PREPARATIONS

With the news reaching Fiengus, who was now back at the University with Bogo, Professor Helmsman, Professor Beeswax and a few others, of the release of the prisoners everyone's spirits were lifted. A plan had been hatched from what they had already gathered and from the fresh revelations Fiengus had gained from Von Staninces. They knew that they would need to go north, somewhere across the sea and that despite what Von Staninces had said they were going to try to stop the arrival of the Legion of Borealis. They agreed that they would need a boat to take them and their equipment and it was agreed that Fiengus, Bogo, Professor Helmsman, Professor Beeswax, Professor Fuirk and Professor Hawks would go. They would take the Machine and head north. The rest of the Feesiks department would continue to observe the skies in hope of catching further sight of the Event, as they were now calling it.

"So we need a boat and we need one quick," said Fiengus to the group.

"Yes and we'll need someone crazy enough to take us there, it is going to be dangerous," added Professor Beeswax.

"Don't worry about that," said Bogo, smiling broadly, "I know just the guy."

They were gathered down at the harbour, with some other professors, who were running last minute checks on the Machine and were gazing at the strangest, wonkiest looking boat they had ever seen and at the oddest looking sailor. He stood before them, a caricature of a sailor; stripy top, a tattoo of a snake; he had even a peg leg. He had the look in his eye that he had been at sea for too long and had forgotten the conventions of society, replaced them with the strange morality that the sea possesses, accompanied by a complete disregard for everyone and anyone who didn't respect it.

"Jeez, all he needs is a parrot," whispered Professor Helmsman to Fiengus, who sniggered a little.

"Thinks it's funny do you that my parrot be gone?" said the surly sailor, sounding distinctly Cornish, "Think that it is funny to be lost out at sea and have to eat your own bird, your one and only friend in the world, because the cruel sea wants it that way. You find that funny?"

Fiengus and Professor Helmsman looked embarrassed and made to apologise when Bogo stepped in, "This is Captain Jake Von Snake and he has agreed to take us on this voyage. We used to sail together a long time ago."

"Before you became a coward," said Captain Jake, sneering at Bogo.

"Yes, and before you became the worst sea captain ever," Bogo retorted, adding "Tell me again, how many ships did you lose?"

The sea captain shifted uneasily, "Well I were cursed, weren't I. The day I threw that poet off my boat into the sea for talking fancy I put a curse on myself. But that was before," he looked at them all individually before continuing, "before I found this," and he pointed to the strange figure head on the prow of the boat. It had a young boys legs on the bottom with a fish on top. "I found this at the bottom of the sea one time. You see I can't drown, it is part of me curse. I had sunk me eighteenth, no it was me twentieth ship, all the crew perished of course, when I saw this on the sea bed. I took it for a sign and brought it back to shore and then attached it to this here boat. The Scurvy Jurky she's called. Ever since, she ain't sunk, it's a blessing, a lifting of me curse." He then walked over and began to stroke the figure head.

"How does this help? It has the legs of a boy and the head of a fish; surely for more effective propulsion through the sea you would want the fish's tail? And you said you found it on the bottom of the sea, which sounds like it was part of a ship then that had sunk. It's not really a good omen then is it?" said an incredulous Professor Helmsman.

The sea Captain stared at him, turning from his beloved figure head, "You sound like that bloody poet, always questioning the mystery of the ocean." Professor Helmsman was about to say something else, when Fiengus interjected, in order to avoid his friend from upsetting the clearly unhinged sea Captain any more.

"Look will you take us then, on your ship, with the, eh, fish-boy at the prow guiding us. It's a dangerous voyage and an even more dangerous destination for us. We could do with all the luck we can get." Fiengus looked at the fish-boy then at the sea captain and smiled, as encouragingly as he could. This was difficult, given the circumstances.

The sea captain looked at him, then turned to look at his ship, "I'll take you, but where exactly are you wanting to go?" he asked.

"We're going north and that is about as much as we know. I'm a feeling that we'll know when we get there," replied Fiengus.

The sea captain gave them all one last look, and then looked at his boat one more time. "Ok, I'll take you. It'll be good to try out the Scurvy Jurky. Load her up then."

"Hang on," said Professor Beeswax suddenly, "you said that this ship had never sunk because of the good omen the fish-boy brings, but you haven't taken it out yet on the sea."

"No, not had a chance, business has been slow for me. You're the first passengers I've had since the last ship I had."

"Well how do you know that the figure head is a good omen?" asked Professor Helmsman.

The sea captain looked confusedly at him, then spat out, "Well of course it is. You weren't there when I found it; it was biblical, like some epic poem. She's sat in this harbour for near a year without sinking and that's better than any of the others." He then turned and began making preparations on the boat, untying ropes, hoisting things up and general maritime type stuff.

Fiengus looked to Professor Helmsman and was thinking that this seemed a doomed mission from the start. This crazy sea captain, who was clearly not meant for sea faring, who was recommended to them by a troll that was brimming with overconfidence and a thirst for danger all seemed to have the aroma of imminent disaster about it. "Professor Helmsman, I've a bad feeling about this one. That boat looks about as buoyant as a sack of bricks and the sea captain as stable as a piece of thread holding them up."

Professor Helmsman looked at him, then out to sea, "I know Fiengus, but we have no choice. We have to do this. It's our only hope." Fiengus refrained from pointing out that if there was one thing they had learned on their adventure, it was that you always had a choice; you couldn't blame fate, divine intervention or anything. It was always your decision and if that decision was to embark on a voyage on a boat that was barely fit for a museum, piloted by a sea captain who you wouldn't trust to look after your toothbrush, then that was your choice and you were responsible. He gazed out to sea and couldn't help wondering what lay out there for them.

23 THE CRUEL MISTRESS

For three days they sailed. For three days they fought the elements, the sea seeming to be against them, as though influenced by a dark force. Professor Hawks was very sea sick and was confined to her cabin. Professor Beeswax had contracted a rare disease and was swollen up like a balloon, while Professor Fuirk had contracted scurvy. Bogo's recklessness was becoming worse and he had narrowly avoided death several times. He had constructed a crow's nest for himself and spent most of his time up there, regardless of the conditions of the sea. Professor Helmsman and Captain Jake Von Snake had expressed their obvious contempt for one another and Fiengus feared that this would come to a head at any moment. A sense of something foreboding and unnatural was washing over them like the salt waves, a feeling that the ship and everyone on board were in fact cursed.

"I can't put up with this much more," said a despondent Professor Helmsman, confiding in Fiengus. "Jake Von Snake is a lunatic. He keeps going on about these insane, ludicrous stories about what he has done." Fiengus nodded in agreement; he knew what the professor was talking about. He had heard Jake Von Snake go on about the mysterious island he had visited, inhabited only by women, who had all fallen in love with him and wanted to make him their king; of how he had in fact been swallowed by a giant sea snake, survived for four months inside its belly before he eventually cut his way out using an old sardine tin opener. This, he said was where he got the idea for tattoo. He said this and much more, telling ever more increasingly unbelievable tales about himself. Each time he told these stories, Professor Helmsman had pointed out why this couldn't be, but Jake Von Snake told him that he didn't understand the mysteries of the sea; he was not one of its chosen ones.

By the fifth day, they had found nothing and everyone was beginning to lose hope. Fiengus and Professor Helmsman were at the prow of the ship looking out to sea, hoping desperately for some sign of the Events coming. Professor Beeswax approached them, still looking like an over inflated beach ball, and explained excitedly that she had heard, through radio, from the professors back at the University that a sighting of a strange phenomena had been made. She told them how one of the younger professors had gone up to the glass observation tower and had bravely sat all night observing the night skies. Just as he was about to give up hope he saw something in the sky and phoned down to report what he had seen. Unfortunately for him the tower, which was very badly in need of repair, suddenly collapsed. The body was never found, being buried under tons of glass. Fiengus had asked how exactly do you not see someone through a pile of glass, but that was apparently what had happened. They had already made plans to erect a new tower and to name it after the recently deceased young professor. She ended by telling them that the professor had seen strange colours in the sky, they were described as swirling and beautiful.

"That's the Northern Lights you're talking about," interrupted Jake Von Snake, who had joined them unnoticed. "They're a sign that the sea is angry with you."

Professor Helmsman looked incredulous, "Aurora Borealis is a natural phenomenon, which has nothing to do with the sea being angry with you. How exactly do you enrage the sea? Forget it's birthday, or tell it that it's mother looks fat?"

Jake Von Snake then moved closer to him and looked him in the eye, "The sea is angry at you for your lack of respect for her. It's you that the sea is angered by, you and your fancy words!" At this a sudden crack filled the air, the sound of thunder. They all looked north and could see an approaching storm. "There I told you so, she demands a sacrifice." At this he leapt forward at Professor Helmsman and grabbed him by the throat and began pushing him towards the end of the boat. Fiengus and Professor Beeswax, struggled with Jake Von Snake, who was as strong as a sea lion. He had a crazed look in his eyes and was staring intently at the professor, who was looking absolutely terrified. Jake Von Snake had him up against the prow now and was holding him over the sea, which was becoming choppier as the storm began to encircle them.

"Stop, Jake, stop!" cried Professor Beeswax.

Fiengus moved a little closer and pleaded with the sea captain, "Look this won't help. This is just a storm, and throwing Professor Helmsman into the sea won't stop it."

Jake Von Snake shot him a glance, "It must be done, the fish-boy demands it!" Just then a flash of lightning shot through the air just above them and hit the mast of the ship, bringing it crashing down. The sea captain let go Professor Helmsman, who had the presence of mind to grab the edge of the ship and pull himself back on board. The sea captain himself was pinned under the mast and was moaning; he seemed strangely calmer than before, the blow to the head causing some sort of sedative effect on him. Bogo, who had been in the crow's nest atop the mast when it fell was laughing at it all, as he picked splinters the size of fingers out of his derriere. Fiengus rushed over to Professor Helmsman and checked if he was alright.

"Yes, I'm fine, as fine as I can be, bearing in mind that I was nearly thrown into the sea by this deranged lunatic sea captain," said a very livid Professor Helmsman. After checking him over quickly and ensuring that no real injury had been done, they looked down at the sea captain and wondered what to do with him.

"We can't leave him like that can we?" asked Professor Beeswax.

"No, but we can't let him loose again. The man's insane and all because of this stupid fish-boy!" replied Professor Helmsman. Jake Von Snake fixed his eyes on him and looked once again enraged.

"That fish-boy is what's keeping us alive, without it the sea would devour us," he cried.

Professor Helmsman looked at him then mockingly went over to the figure head and began pretending to pray to it. "Oh thank you oh mighty, fish-boy for keeping us safe. Why without you our ramshackle junk would not be fit for the sea with such a worthy sea captain as is Jake Von Snake," at this he leaned onto the fish-boy and looked at Jake Von Snake. "Well, what is going to happen now? Will the sea forgive me for thinking like a rational person instead of a superstitious fish wife?" As he said this he slapped the fish-boy mockingly and smiled as he turned. Fiengus and Professor Beeswax let out a scream and rushed to the prow, they got their just in time to see the fish-boy figure head fall from the ship and sink into the sea. "Oh crap," said Professor Helmsman, turning to look at the sea captain.

Jake Von Snake let out a terrible cry of pain and anguish. The others stepped back from him as he kicked and screamed on the floor. He suddenly threw the mast off himself, displaying superhuman strength and rushed to the end of the boat and leapt into the sea. The others looked over the edge, but could not see him; he was gone, swallowed up by the cruel, briny mistress, whom he was at one now. The ship then began to make loud and worrying creaking and cracking sounds. The storm had picked up around them almost unnoticed, but now they could see that the sky had gone an impenetrable dark grey and the wind was now howling, causing the sea to swell around them. Professor Hawks and Professor Fuirk came rushing up from below deck and cried, "We're taking on water the ship is sinking!" They all looked at Professor Helmsman, who was looking very sheepish.

"Oh you can't believe that this is happening because I knocked the fish-boy off the ship? Really?" The doubt was apparent in his voice and so was the fear. The ship was beginning to sink and there was nothing they could do. They were desperately trying to pail water from the ship, but it was all to no avail. Water was now coming up on deck and they were forced to climb onto the roof of the wheel house and were quite reasonably upset about it all. Just when it looked like all hope was lost the clouds suddenly parted, revealing a cone of sunlight and a winged figure that swept down on them. The figure grabbed hold of the ship and began pulling it out of the water.

What happened next passed like a dream to them all. They could remember the ship being carried by the figure through the air, beyond the clouds and the storm, revealing a blue sky above the tumultuous clouds below, which bore resemblance to the sea that had almost claimed each of their lives. Eventually they were set down on a cliff, on what appeared to be a small island. They were all truly in shock and before anyone could utter a word the figure flew away without saying anything.

Some time passed before anyone spoke. It was Bogo who broke the silence, "We need to do that again!" The others looked at him and laughed too. They were all very much relieved to be alive.

After checking their equipment and establishing that everything and everyone was ok they began to set up a small camp for the night. Tents were erected and a small fire was going, around which they were making a meal. They were discussing what had happened and reliving the experience. They were only just beginning to realise what had actually happened to them.

"Who do you think that was? The winged figure that picked us out of the sea and carried us and an entire ship onto this island," asked Professor Fuirk.

"I think that I recognise him from somewhere," replied Fiengus.

"Fiengus, you always think you have met people before," said Professor Helmsman.

"No, really, he reminded me of that guy who kidnapped you, the strange little guy with the Humphrey Bogart thing going on," replied Fiengus.

"You know what you're right; he did remind me of him. Remember he had something hidden underneath his jacket. It could have been wings," said Bogo. "I remember him being really strong too, when we fought," he added.

"It's so strange," said Fiengus, "that he tried to kill us before and now he comes to save us like that. Maybe he was trying to make amends by doing that. To think he might be up there now," said Fiengus, looking up to the stars which were now visible. "Hey look," he said excitedly, rising from the ground. They all looked up and saw the dancing, swirling greens and blues of the Northern Lights; Aurora Borealis. It was directly above them and making its way down to the island.

"That's weird," said Professor Helmsman, "Aurora Borealis shouldn't be moving that way. It's supposed to reflect off the earth's atmosphere, the thermosphere, which causes the light we see, but this is moving straight down. It's getting closer." The others were noticing this too; the lights were heading down to a part of the island further inland.

"You don't think this is it, do you? The coming of the Legion of Borealis. Actually, now that I think about it the name the Legion of Borealis, it has to be!" said Professor Fuirk. The others were looking around, unsure of what to do. Only one of them seemed to have any presence of mind; Bogo Snot Troll.

He climbed up onto a rock and roared out to the others, "This is it! This is our moment, what we've been leading up to. The chance to destroy the Legion of Borealis, what we've waited to do all our lives!"

"Well, not really all our lives. We only heard about the Legion last week," said Professor Beeswax.

"True," replied Bogo, "but it is still very important that we stop them."

The others agreed with this. "Grab the Machine, we've got a world to save," cried out Fiengus, who enjoyed the impressed looks he received from the others. He decided to add to the impression by walking steadfastly away. However, he stopped several metres away and turned around, "It's this way isn't it?" he asked.

They made their way inland, following the now steady stream of light that was descending from the heavens onto the island. They were marching up hill, making a steady ascent from the coastal cliffs. At the top they gained a clearer view and could now see where the spiralling column of light was meeting the island. It was somewhere on what seemed to be a small mountain. Up ahead they saw a staircase that had been hewn from the rock itself and led up the side of the mountain. They followed the stairs and made their way to the top. Once there they passed through a huge archway, which was missing a large portion, but still remained standing though precariously. When they were through it they all gazed in awe at a magnificent city, which was, despite being very badly burned and large parts completely destroyed, truly majestic. There was a thick layer of ash that lay strewn upon the ground. In the centre of the city, some way into it, the light was coming down.

"What is this place?" asked Bogo.

"I don't know," replied Fiengus, "but it seems that the light is coming down not too far from here." They then continued on through the deserted city. They passed down streets that were flanked by impressive buildings, which looked as though they were made of marble, though it was hard to tell with the damage. They continued on some way, and then found their way blocked by a large tower which had fallen and now blocked their route. The only thing to do was to climb in by one of the windows and make their way through.

They entered the tower and felt immediately disorientated. Walking through a building on its side has this effect. As they scrambled over broken and scorched furniture they eventually made it to the other side. The window through which they exited the tower led into a palatial garden, though nothing grew there anymore; it was apparent to even the most unimaginative person that this must have been a very special place. Fiengus imagined the varieties of exotic plants that would have been here; the fountain that would have cascaded water, creating a soothing and serene sound through the gardens, but was now a charred remain.

"What happened here?" asked Professor Fuirk, looking around.

"It looks like a volcanic eruption, what with all the ash and terrible fire damage to everything," answered Professor Helmsman.

As they made their way through the garden they noticed that in the centre of the waterless fountain was a winged statue, bearing an uncanny resemblance to the one that had saved them. No one commented, but they all had the same conclusion. They stopped at the far end of the garden, at a doorway that led to the other side of the very large wall that circumvented the gardens. On the other side the light was coming into contact with the ground and their fate awaited them. Doubt hit everyone suddenly and hard, even Bogo was feeling it.

"Are we really about to face one of the most powerful forces in the universe armed with only a tape deck, with a small screen on it and a collection of popular music?" asked Fiengus.

"I'm supposed to dance in order to enhance the powerful effects of this Karaoke machine using a dance mat I stole from my brother's console system," added Professor Beeswax.

"It really does sound stupid doesn't it, when you put it like that," said Professor Helmsman. He then laughed, "But hey, what have we got to lose? I've seen a lot of stranger things and heard of far stranger."

"He's right; we didn't come all this way for nothing. This might seem absolutely ridiculous, but we've got to try," added Bogo, suddenly feeling more himself, well at least the self he had been lately.

"Sod it, let's just get in there!" cried Fiengus, who grabbed the Machine and turned it on. At this they left the garden and ventured forth.

On the other side they could see the light which was coming down. They were in what was like a large amphitheatre made of marble. What immediately struck them all was that this whole area seemed untouched by the devastation that engulfed the rest of the city. It was pristine white, the marble shone in the eerie glow of Aurora Borealis. Looking up the column they could see figures slowly descending, they looked to be around a thousand feet from the ground. This was it; this was the Legion of Borealis. They were just about to wish each other luck when Fiengus' phone began to ring.

"Who is it?" asked Professor Helmsman.

Fiengus looked at the screen and said, "I don't recognise the number. Should I answer? It might be important." The others agreed and Fiengus answered, "Hello?" A voice began talking, the others could not make out what was being said. "No I'm not interested in changing my broadband provider, look this really isn't the time. No, I don't get unlimited usage; I don't use the internet enough..." Bogo grabbed Fiengus' phone from him and hung up. "Thanks Bogo, I can never get rid of these people." He looked at the angry faces glaring at him, "Look sorry, let's fire up the Machine then."

What happened next was an onslaught of back to back hits delivered with the force of a neutron bomb. Various tracks were played, each with all the gusto and enthusiasm they could muster. Bogo and Fiengus helmed the microphones, Professor Beeswax, despite her corpulence, danced phenomenally. Professor Helmsman did a solo rendition of Neil Diamond's *Sweet Caroline*, followed by a stalwart rendition of *Sweet Child o' Mine* by Professor Fuirk. Track after track were being played, producing phenomenal power, but it was not until Fiengus and Bogo once again manned the microphones for the finale, the coup de grace, ABBA's *Thank You for the Music* that an obvious affect could be seen on the Aurora Borealis. It began to fade slightly, and then started to flash. The Legion, who had continued to descend suddenly, began to wail out. Whatever it was they were doing it was working. The column suddenly began to fade and ascend back up to the stars, slowly at first and then more quickly At the final few bars of the song a sudden explosion occurred and a blinding white light shot out. The flash was so bright that the huge crowd that had gathered on the dock of Von Dufflestein could see it.

The arena lay silent. Fiengus and his companions were just beginning to pick themselves up from the ground. Fiengus looked up and cried out, "We've done it! We won!" The others joined him in celebration; the column of light was gone, the Event had been stopped. There was much cheering and hugging and celebrating. The people on Von Dufflestein pier were celebrating too; they had seen the column shoot back up and then disappear and knew that they had been saved. Professor Helmsman made his way over to the Machine and peered down at it. The piece of tape that held the deck on had given out and the cassette was completely destroyed, it's ribbon spewed out. The Machine had served its purpose, but was now beyond repair.

Fiengus took out his phone and dialled the Mayor's office. The receptionist answered, "We've done it," Fiengus said with immense pride. "Tell the Mayor that we have stopped the Event and that we want to go home."

"Well done, we were all just talking about you. He'll be very pleased, we'll all be really pleased," she replied. She sounded truly enamoured, thought Fiengus.

He then added, "Me and you should get dinner when I come

back. How about it?" He looked to Bogo, who winked at him.

"You sly old dog," Bogo said to him.

The receptionist paused for a second before giving her response, "Probably not, I'm married you see." Fiengus felt slightly crestfallen. He returned his phone to his pocket.

"No was it?" asked Professor Helmsman. "Well, you did just save the world. One thing at a time, eh?" Fiengus looked up and then smiled.

"I did just save the world, we all did. We are bloody brilliant!" At this they all cheered again.

The group then went back to the cliff and awaited being collected. Eventually a grand and fine ship was sent to collect them, with an emotionally stable captain who warmly welcomed them aboard. The journey back to Von Dufflestein, was uneventful and Fiengus spent most of it wondering what he would do now. He made a decision; there was something that he needed to do, something that he had put off for some time.

24 DENOUMENT

After returning to Von Dufflestein the group were heroes. They had saved the town using Karaoke and had stopped the Legion of Borealis. They attended parties, press conferences, were invited to appear on television, did magazine interviews. Bogo and Fiengus were even approached to record a single and Professor Helmsman was offered a modelling contract. The tirade of publicity and public attention was overwhelming and eventually the group decided to part ways for a bit, to return to a bit of normality. Professors Fuirk and Hawkes returned to the University and began work on one of Professor Nigel's research projects. Sadly they have both been missing, having attempted to disprove gravity at 20,000 feet. On a positive note the young professor, who had observed Aurora Borealis was found. He had apparently been living it up in Hawaii, having come into some money through a life insurance policy. Sadly he now faces a very serious law suit against him back in Von Dufflestein. As to the naming of the tower, it looks as though it won't be named after him after all.

Professor Beeswax decided that she was going to go solo from the University for a bit and created her own dance school. Unfortunately the swelling from the rare disease she caught on board the cursed Scurvy Jurky never settled and she was forced to abandon her dancing career and returned to the University to conduct research into the motions of incredibly large objects.

Bogo decided that he couldn't return to his family again, not in his current state of extreme bravery and dare devilishness. He went instead in search of peace and solitude and hopefully the opportunity to regain some of his cowardice, which had made him so popular with the other trolls before. It was rumoured that he had been journeying in the mountains and met with the Monk and was spending time trying to find himself.

Professor Helmsman initially went back to the University, but after huge sales of his until then unsuccessful book and the offer of an accompanying TV programme, he left the University for a sabbatical. He grew fond of the limelight that Fiengus had grown to loathe his celebrity status was something that he revelled in. Fiengus on the other hand decided that he wanted away from it all and, ironically it seemed to him, returned to the place he had been running from for his whole life, the place he had been trying to define himself in contrast to; his family home.

On the drive up, the house being situated several miles out of Von Dufflestein, he caught his first glimpse of his family home in many years. He thought how it looked worse than ever. All that remained of the once magnificent castle was the west tower, which sat now at a precarious angle. The rest of the house had either collapsed from disrepair or had been sold on. The Longfinger family had been a great family once, had owned much of the land surrounding the town and had even been intrinsic in the inception of the town itself. However, as the generations came they steadily became more and more reluctant to do anything, living off the backs of their forefathers, resulting in the family being regarded as a joke within the town and renowned for their indolence. This was what Fiengus had rebelled against when he was younger, what had caused the still extant rift in the family. They just couldn't understand 'why he wanted to do anything so common as doing something.'

He felt all this come flooding back to him as he got out of the car and gazed up at the still impressive, in terms of its height, tower. It did however look ready to come falling down at any moment. Swallowing down the nerves he felt, he approached the door and rang the bell; he was not expected, as far as he knew. He was about to turn away when the door opened and a voice he hadn't heard for some time greeted him most welcomingly, "Master Fiengus, is that you? Why it is. Come in, come in. Oh but it is your house, you don't need me to invite you." Fiengus turned around and gazed at the family's faithful butler, Gilles the Housekeeper Spider. He was looking almost fatherly at Fiengus through all 32 of his eyes, and Fiengus could swear that in at least one of them a tear was forming.

"It's not my house anymore Gilles, hasn't been for a long time. I've missed you," he said and embraced the spider, who wasn't like a normal spider, in several respects. Firstly he was much larger than a regular spider, about the size of a child. Secondly, he did not eat insects and took great offense at the suggestion. He was in fact a highly trained chef, who had a superior palate and regarded himself as a bit of a food snob. There were many other differences, which don't need mentioning, that became more apparent the more you got to know him. Gilles threw down his feather duster, spray polish, packet of doilies, today's newspaper, rubber plunger, bottle of bleach and embraced Fiengus. There could be no doubt; several of Gilles' eyes were filling with tears.

"Well I suppose you're here to see the family then," said Gilles after picking up his things.

"Yes I suppose so," replied Fiengus who received a knowing look from Gilles.

They ascended the spiralling staircase that made its way up the tower, talking about Fiengus' recent exploits. Gilles was particularly impressed that Fiengus had used Karaoke to defeat the Legion of Borealis, and remarked that this was something he would have never have thought of. The interior of the tower was adorned with the bare minimum of decoration and was barely lit by the sparse lighting provided by a few lamps placed here and there. Fiengus thought to himself how different it looked from when he had been young; it had once been resplendent with tapestries, coats of arms, suits of armour, all variety of curiosities befitting castle chic. Eventually they made it to the topmost room, which had a closed door. The room sounded silent, perhaps in anticipation of his arrival.

They entered what was a more opulently decorated room, in fact one done out in a very over the top manner. Every wall, table, piece of floor space seemed to be overwhelmed with various paintings, tapestries, ornaments, statues all in a miss mash of incongruity, creating a disconcerting effect on Fiengus, causing him to barely notice his family sitting around a large table eating a meal. His brother, Gunter was wearing a bizarre looking hat resplendent with an incredibly large feather with a bright orange suit. He was incredibly fat these days, though he had always been portly. Barely acknowledging Fiengus' entrance he gave a perfunctory nod in his direction then continued to gorge himself on roast chicken. His father sat at one end of the table and cast a glance, which could easily have been mistaken for hostility, but said nothing.

His mother was the one to break the silence. She put down her cutlery, wiped her mouth with a threadbare silken napkin and then half turned to face Fiengus, remaining in her chair. "So you're back eh? The prodigal son returns, seeking out gratification, forgiveness? Which is it?" she said scornfully.

Fiengus thought he would tackle all three questions at once, "Yes I am back and it's not for any of these reasons... it's for another reason actually. More for your benefit than for me really."

"Oh the hilarity of it!" said his mother sardonically, the other two laughing along too. "How are you to help us exactly?"

Fiengus looked at them. They hadn't changed one bit, apart from looking older and a little fatter. "It's this, it's all of it," he said looking around the room, "the way you live your life. You live in this derelict remnant of a castle and hide away from the world; the people in the town make jokes about you."

"They laugh at us? I heard you have become a karaoke singer," said his mother, "And they laugh at us!" She looked around the table for approval.

"This is your ancestral home. How dare you talk of it this way. The Longfinger's have lived in this castle for 15 generations and you have the audacity to speak of it as a ruin, a relic," said his father, who had turned from his food to his son. "The painting on that wall there could buy half the town. What do we care about them? They owe us allegiance. Our forefathers built this town!" he continued enraged now.

"You have no idea what you have done to your father; he's wept himself to sleep thinking about you being a karaoke singer. And now you come here and criticise us!" Added his mother.

His brother then turned to Fiengus, having finished his very generous portion of chicken and said, "Hey Fiengus, how are you?" he smiled at his brother. He then turned to his mother and said "Can I go to my room now?" She nodded and he left through a door, waving to Fiengus as he left. His brother had always been one not to take sides and had found it difficult growing up with an opinionated brother who disagreed with most of what his parents did and said and thought.

"You've upset your brother too," said his mother. Fiengus was getting a little annoyed now at the constant barrage of insults and accusations being thrown at him.

"Oh enough," he shouted, which took them by surprise, "You go on about this family's great and grand lineage, yet you lot have done nothing! My brother is a grown man who stills asks permission to go to his bedroom after his meal!"

"Look, Henry, he hates his brother now too!" rebuked his mother, with feigned indignation. "You leave him out of this, the poor sweet gentle boy; at least he doesn't bring the family name to such disgrace."

"Poor sweet boy? He's 36 years old! You lot do nothing, live off the back of the family name, the great deeds done hundreds of years ago. I have done something, I at least try to do something!"

"He did save Von Dufflestein from imminent danger," added Gilles, who was shot a glance from Fiengus' mother. The father looked at him, then to Fiengus.

"Yes and a great lot of good that did. These *Instances* that you were supposed to have stopped have begun happening again in Von Dunkenstein," said his father, then turning to the mother added, "I read about it in the newspaper." He then picked up a newspaper and pointed to the headlines,

Instances happening again! The story then mentioned how a local of Von Dunkenstein, one Von Bigentow, had witnessed an *Instance*. Fiengus had read this, the man was a professor from the University of Von Dunkenstein and had discredited the work they had done on Karaoke and said that it had been reckless and had ultimately failed in stopping the *Instances*. He had then went on to trivialise their research and call into question their scientific methods, even going so far as to claim them to be 'populist sensationalists.'

This had irritated Fiengus at the time; he loathed the celebrity status that he seemed to have been branded with and was annoyed at how quickly people had turned on them after all they had done.

"You see, a lot of twaddle all this Karaoke and Feesiks you lot are involved in," resumed his father.

Fiengus had had enough. His family just weren't going to be swayed by reason. They were beyond hope and yet still he loved them. Despite his every effort he was always going to be defined against them. He said goodbye to them all and his father walked him to the door.

"Well, son, hope to see you soon. It was lovely catching up and seeing you again. Your mother is always talking about you. She wants what's best for you, you know," said his father. Fiengus was taken aback by this, even though every time they argued his father seemed to think that was how things were meant to be done. They truly believed that what they were doing was for the best and that at some time he would eventually see things their way, the proper Longfinger way. "You look different, it's like you have changed. Be wary of change Fiengus; it is always accompanied by the unexpected." They then said their goodbyes and Fiengus got in his car and left, watching the road ahead intently.

He eventually reached a crossroads and came to a stop. The road was intersected by several others, giving a number of possible routes for him to take. He looked out and saw the sun beginning to set, signalling the end of the day, but bringing the promise of another to come. He sat thinking about what he should do, where he should go; the existential feeling he had had was still there, but he accepted that it always would be, that it was a good thing to have, a constant yearning and desire to find new paths in life and new ways of being. The feeling of freedom that he felt he had in making the choices in his own life both excited and terrified him. Leaning back in his chair he reached into the glove box and took out his sat-nav and turned it on. The voice indicated that he should go straight ahead. He put the car in to gear and was just about to go when he changed his mind. He pulled the car onto the verge of the road, turned off the engine and got out. He looked once more to the fading sun, then looked all around him and felt everything. Fiengus Longfinger then left the road and began walking, making his own path in an unfamiliar territory.

ABOUT THE AUTHOR

This is the first book by G.W. Witherspoon. He expressly hopes you enjoyed it. If you have (or if you haven't) please contact him at:

thegwwitherspoon@gmail.com

You can also follow him on Twitter:
@witherspoon_w

CPSIA information can be obtained at www.ICGtesting.com
Printed in the USA
LVOW06s2143140915

454106LV00005B/726/P